Closing Costs
Stewart Realty Book 3
By Liz Crowe

This is a work of fiction. Similarities to real people, places, or events are entirely coincidental.

CLOSING COSTS

First edition. May 5, 2024.

Copyright © 2024 Liz Crowe.

ISBN: 979-8224858484

Written by Liz Crowe.

Prologue

Sara struggled to throw off the blanket, to open her eyes, to get her feet to the floor—anything to get out from under the smothering darkness enveloping her. She tried holding her eyes open with her fingers, but that didn't work. Counting to three and heaving herself up and out of the bed didn't either. She simply could not move.

Everything smelled funny. Sort of like the rubber gloves her mother used to keep under the sink for the dreaded cleaning marathons of her youth. The gloves were tight, hot, and gross. They were from her parents' medical practice, designed to peel off and toss when the task was finished, but the weird, sweaty rubbery odor would linger for days no matter how much soap she used.

Why was she so thirsty? Dear God, her throat was like the Mohave Desert in a drought.

The dried out rivulets of flesh in the back of her mouth were slimed in a disgusting, coppery, medicinal ooze. But the thirst—it was like a live thing, crouching in her gut. And the saliva that coated her mouth only made it worse, teasing her with nauseating dampness. She moaned and threw a hand over her face as lights flooded her bedroom.

Something held her back. Wires or maybe restraints.

Did Jack do this? After all these months of avoidance, had he talked her into the sex play they used to enjoy back when they could still stand the sight of each other? Something about that thought brought tears to her eyes.

That's when it caught up with her—massive capital letter "P" Pain, cutting her in half.

"Help!" she yelled. But it came out as a weak croak. She was still trying to sort out why her bedroom looked like a hospital room, why there were not one but two IVs stuck in her, one in her left hand, the other currently straining against the inside of her right elbow and quickly filling with blood. "Somebody, I'm gonna..."

Two women appeared, dressed in annoyingly bright pink scrubs, one dotted with—Sara strained her eyes just before she puked into the plastic kidney bean shaped container—Hello Kitty faces. Tears streamed down her face as she flopped back.

"Is it possible to throw up your pancreas? I think I just did." Hello Kitty nurse hustled out as the other one fussed around with her IV, took her pulse and temperature.

"What's your pain on a scale of one to ten?"

Sara tried to hold her eyes open, to remain this side of conscious, but slipped slowly back under as she whispered: "Forty-five," remembering too late she still needed a drink of water.

"Sara."

A disembodied hand patted hers. Sara gasped, tried to sit, terror gripping her chest. When her gaze met a pair of familiar, soft green eyes, tears slipped down her cheeks. Agony blossomed from every inch of her body. She lay back, gingerly, thinking if she curled in on herself and hid, the pain wouldn't find her.

"Honey, want me to call a nurse?" her mother asked. Sara shut her eyes. There was something in the woman's arms—something she kept looking at. "Do you want to see her, Sara? Your daughter—she's so beautiful."

She did. But she hurt, like, everywhere. It felt as though she'd been in a major car accident and not done the most natural thing on earth. Even if she could barely remember the details of it. Other than there was, indeed, a daughter who needed her.

"How long have I been in here?" Her dry lips split. "Can I have some water?" She could barely hear her own voice as the pain ripped through her again. "Jack?"

He didn't materialize. And her mother had faded on her. The best defense seemed to be passing out. So she did.

"Okay Sleeping Beauty, enough already." A firm voice pierced the fuzz that was packed around her brain. Dark brown eyes met hers as she fought to the surface again. "C'mon, there's someone here that wants to meet you," Craig insisted.

Craig. Why was he here? Oh, right, he'd been there when I bled all over the conference room floor. Not to mention when this kid had been conceived.

Sara sighed and stretched, wincing when she found something like a million muscles that were sore.

"Water. Can I please get some?" Blake appeared on her other side, a white cup in one hand. The glorious liquid soothed her throat. She gulped and gulped until Blake took it from her.

"Slow down." His deep green eyes were red rimmed, but he smiled and she relaxed.

"Now, let me present you with Miss Katherine Elizabeth Thornton." Craig stuck a pink-blanketed bundle in the crook of her arm. The bundle shifted. A mewling sound came from its depths. Sara gasped as a sudden mild tingling in her breasts became a fresh roar of agony. Her mouth dried out again so fast she whimpered. The baby wiggled and made more noises. Sara tried very hard not to panic.

The almost nine months she'd spent pregnant were interminable. But she'd gotten adjusted to being the preggers princess, despite all the discomforts and various medical dramas it provoked. The concept that there would be a small, helpless human to care for at the end of it had become a distant thought, an idea or a possibility that right now, she held in her arms.

And she'd never been more terrified about anything in her life.

At that moment, a woman strode in, took the baby and declared herself the "lactation coach," dismissing Craig and Blake from the room. Sara stared at her, one hand over her aching boob.

"I thought this was a natural act. Why do I need a coach? I didn't need a coach to get in this condition. Ow!" The woman pulled one side of Sara's hospital gown down with no preamble or warning, exposing a giant, leaking breast. "Holy shit, that hurts!"

She tried to flinch away, but the crazy woman kept holding her freakishly giant tit, rubbing her leaky nipple against the baby's cheek. It took about three seconds for the kid to latch on. "Jesus!" Sara winced, bent over, trying not to smother her own child during her first few hours as a mother.

"That's it." The evil torturer smiled. "Perfect. You two are naturals at this."

"Water?" Sara whimpered.

The woman handed her the cup. "You'll want to always have water around as you nurse."

"No shit," Sara muttered, as the painful tugging at her nipple increased, then settled into a soft rhythm. She leaned back and sighed, finally taking a peek down at her baby. The girl's huge eyes were open and locked on her with an unnerving intensity. Then her tiny, perfect face broke into a grin around Sara's nipple. When she curled her small body tighter against Sara's body, a surge of something she'd never experienced in her entire life shot through her then. A strange, visceral energy that started in her scalp and worked its way down her spine, lighting up every nerve ending she possessed.

She smiled down at Katherine Elizabeth.

Her daughter.

I will be the perfect mother.

I'll read you books every night, only serve you organically grown non-junk food your entire life, and always listen to you. I'll be home every day when you get in from school with homemade cookies and plenty of time to sit and hear about your day. I'll take you to dance lessons, piano, violin, anything you want.

She ran her fingertip down the impossibly small nose, making the girl flinch and lose her concentration. She glared at her mother for a split second.

The look spoke volumes.

"You won't either," she seemed to accuse. "You'll work too many hours. I'll be a latchkey kid, and an evil, pot-smoking adolescent, and we'll do nothing but fight."

A goofy smile-like thing Sara knew was likely gas lit the girl's face.

"But it's okay. I'll love you, anyway."

A fresh surge of anxiety gripped Sara's throat as the child nursed a bit more, then slept. Sara stared at her, watched a bit of thin-looking, white liquid drip from the girl's open mouth. Feeling like the world's biggest idiot, she held on tight, unsure of what the hell do to next.

Would her coach show back up? Give her a high-five and send her to the showers? Waves of emotion pounded in her brain, as her pain level ramped back up now that endorphins had stopped flowing.

"Sara?"

She looked up, confused at the sight of Jack's tall frame filling the doorway. He was dressed in jeans and a polo. His face looked gaunt. His blue eyes were bloodshot and full of worry. She sucked in a breath and glanced back down at the girl who'd fallen asleep at her breast, sucked in a breath, and burst into tears.

He was at her side in a split second, holding tight as sobs racked her. "I'm sorry. I don't know why I'm crying," she choked out as she readjusted the baby to her other arm and tried to shove her still massive boob back into her gown. Jack plucked a tissue from a nearby box and tried to hand it to her. She shook her head. "I'm afraid to let go of her." Her voice cracked. He shrugged and held the tissue to her nose.

"Blow."

She did as he said. He disposed of the tissue and climbed up on the bed beside her. She snuggled into his side, relief making her giggle.

Dear God, these hormones are worse than the pregnancy ones.

"You look like hell, my dear." He put a tentative hand on the baby, then drew back as she stirred. Sara stiffened, but he tightened his arm around her shoulders.

"Everything's okay. Baby's good. You made it, thank God." He pressed his lips to her temple. "We weren't sure for a while. Although a shower might be a good idea…"

"I can't do this," she whispered, still gripping the child close. "I can barely take care of myself. What made me think…? Oh Jesus." Tears kept leaking down her face. Jack held her closer. "Ow. Sorry. I hurt all over."

He moved the pink blanket aside. The baby startled. Sara saw something like fear flicker in his eyes. Her arm was getting sore from staying in one position for long. But having Jack here holding her felt better than anything, and she didn't want the moment to end. "So much for all those Lamaze hours, huh? I didn't even need them."

"Time wasted indeed. Way to scare everybody, drama queen." He stayed quiet for a while. "Listen, Sara, you can do this. You made it through months of crazy medical bullshit, worked, bought a new house, moved. All of it. You'll be fine."

"But Jack." She hated the sound of her own whine. "I don't know what to do with her. I mean, how do I get her home? How does she sleep? Where does she sleep?"

"You have a complete library of how-to books. Didn't you read any of them? And, if I remember right, painting this kid's nursery almost cost us our friendship. So I'm pretty sure she has a place to sleep."

Sara tried not to let the word "friendship" bug her too much. She'd insisted on keeping it that way, after all.

"Well, I sort of only skimmed the books," she said by way of deflection as she stared down at her sleeping baby. Her daughter. Katie. The reason she'd pushed both Jack and Craig out of her life for good, in a strange fit of somewhat misplaced independence—or stubbornness.

"They're saying you guys can go home at the end of the week. I'll help. I mean, you know if your posse out there will let me." He ran a shaking hand through his hair, then stared at the baby, that weird look in his eyes again.

"We'll be the blind leading the blind. Who would have thought a baby would scare you?" He sighed and seemed to deflate. She cursed herself for ruining a perfectly pleasant moment.

"Something like that. But I gotta go. Hospitals make me antsy and you've got a virtual arsenal of people out there dying to get in here and help you. None of them were too happy about my presence."

She let familiar anger grip her, pushing the abject terror at going home with the human being in her arms out of her head for a minute.

"Go on. I'll call you."

He stood and shoved his hands in his pockets. "You wanted it this way, remember? Just you and her," he said, reminding her of her stupid words, spoken out of anger at herself for getting knocked up in the first place, like some ignorant teenager who didn't know any better.

"I know." She looked down to hide the tears that kept forming. "So go." She glanced back up at him, the man she loved but refused to admit it, and bit back the urge to beg him to stay with her. She'd set the parameters, and he was honoring them. End of story. End of her possible happily ever after, nuclear family, mom, dad, baby life. She squared her shoulders to hide how shitty she felt, knowing he was doing exactly what she'd told him to do.

"Thanks for the pep talk. I got this."

His smile was half-hearted. He moved away from her when there was at a knock on the door.

"Come in," she called out. "Jack was just leaving." By the time he'd walked out, Sara realized too late that she never even asked if he wanted to hold the baby.

Chapter One

Seven Months Earlier

Sara stared out the window and willed the ever-present nausea away. Blake put a hand on her shoulder, making her jump. She resisted the urge to step away. She was antsy, didn't want anyone touching her, even her brother.

"You sure you don't want me here for this?"

She nodded, biting her lip, watching for the two familiar cars to pull into her condo community lot. When they did, panic wrapped tight cords around her chest. She made a dash for the bathroom, dry heaving for the millionth time that day. While she was rinsing out her mouth, she heard Blake greet both Craig and Jack, their deep voices mixing, filling her small space.

Glancing in the mirror over the sink, she sighed.

I'd give anything to be somewhere, anywhere, else right now.

Her reflection mocked her with its unhelpful silence. She turned at a soft knock on the door, and saw her brother standing in the doorway.

"I'm coming," she whispered. Blake gave her a quick hug, then gripped her arms and stared into her eyes.

"You can do this. You know Mom and Dad understand. They get it. We're all behind you. Now go out there and tell them both what you invited them over to hear. It's the only way. You've been avoiding them both since the end of the year. Time to woman up."

She nodded, and leaned into him for a moment. Blake had always been there for her. She really wanted him to stay, but she had to do this – have this conversation – alone.

"I could crawl in bed right now and sleep for hours." She pulled back, ran a hand over her eyes. "I feel like an alien version of myself. I hate it." He put an arm around her shoulders and guided her out to the living room, kissed her forehead and slipped out the front door without another word.

She paused, watching the two men as they sat at her small dining room table. Jack Gordon, tall, ruggedly handsome in his dark suit, staring at his smart phone, blue eyes glittering with concentration. Craig Robinson, his easy, loose-limbed frame draped over a nearby chair, in khakis and an ever-wrinkled-yet-somehow-perfect button down, deep brown eyes staring right at her. She gave him a weak smile and stepped into the room.

"I'm pregnant."

They blinked and their mouths fell open in unison. If it weren't so god awful, it would be hilarious. She sat, put her shaking hands on her knees, and stayed quiet. Saliva flooded her mouth, announcing an impending bout of puke, but she kept it at bay. Jack spoke first.

"Who's the father?" He glanced at Craig then back at her. "I assume we're both here so you can fill us in on that minor detail."

Craig leaned forward on his knees. "How're you feeling?"

God these guys were so predictable.

She directed her first response to Jack, fighting back to urge to throw herself at him, to be enveloped in his arms, turn the whole thing over to him and let him take care of her.

"I don't know which of you is the father." She turned to Craig, let the sunny warmth of his concern give her strength and kept her voice firm. "I feel like warmed over shit most days, thanks. On the other days, I want to sleep twenty-four seven. Being pregnant sucks so far."

Jack got up and started pacing the room. She tried to keep the anger out of her voice.

"Look, I didn't want this either but..."

"You aren't doing anything...permanent about that are you?" He stared out the window as he spoke.

"If you're asking me if I'm considering an abortion, Jack, the answer is no. Not anymore anyway." He whirled to face her. His gaze held something she refused to acknowledge—something that bordered on relief. She forced herself to look away. "The bottom line is, as you have likely sorted out by now, either of you could have...could be..." She gulped back a surge of nausea so strong she had to rush from the room.

A few minutes later, she leaned on the doorjamb of her bathroom and tried to will away the creeping exhaustion gripping her again.

How in the hell did I get here? All those times without condoms? Fucking careless and stupid.

Her self-flagellation ended when she heard Craig's voice.

"Sara?" She tried not to cry at the expression on his face. "Oh honey, I'm, sorry. Or whatever. I don't know what to say, really." He pulled her into his arms. She sucked in a breath of him – chlorine, cotton, a whiff of the clean linen of his cologne. He led her back to the kitchen table.

"It's okay Sara. It'll all be fine," he declared. She tried to dry up the waterworks, forced herself out of the comforting circle of Craig's arms and wiped her hand across her eyes. After taking a breath, she looked at them both.

"I'm doing this on my own."

Craig stepped back. Jack crossed his arms. "And you mean what by that exactly?"

"I mean that I won't be getting a paternity test. I don't care who did this." She stopped and attempted to sound less strident. "Which one of you knocked me up is irrelevant. It's my body and my baby. I'm telling you both now that we can be friends, all of us, but that's it. I will handle this from here on out. Period."

Suddenly thirsty, she brushed past them, heading for the kitchen. After gulping down a large glass of water, she turned to face them again. Her men. The light and dark. The yin and yang of her entire existence.

Was she doing the right thing? Was it fair to them? Or was she letting her family railroad her into taking this stand? She suddenly had no idea what she was doing anymore. But the words were out of her mouth now, and they continued to stare at her, a similar incredulity lining their faces.

"You realize how ridiculous that sounds, right?" Jack stood, feet apart, arms crossed, the posture she remembered well from their brief and ill-fated foray into life as an engaged and living-together couple. It was his fighting stance. She tried not to rise to the bait. She looked at Craig, hoping he would defuse it, but he stayed silent. "Right?" Jack repeated, his voice dipping low, making her scalp tingle.

She shook herself. This was not some sex game. This was her new reality. And as her brother said, she had to woman up and take responsibility for it. All of it. Despite the temptation to point to one of the men staring at her from across the kitchen and say "It's you. Now, do the right thing by me," she knew better. This had to be her moment to break clean from them both. It was the only way she could cope with how she felt about them both.

"Honestly, Sara, Jack may be right." Both she and the tall man in the suit looked at Craig. He ignored Jack and kept his gaze trained on her. "You can't pretend that we don't care. I mean I know if it's my, um, child, I would…you know, take some responsibility."

"Yeah," Jack sputtered, his face turning red. Sara frowned. "I have, I mean, we, well, one of us has some rights here."

A crisp, clean and likely irrational fury made her vision blur. "Really. And what right would that be, Jack? The right to hold my hair while I puke my ever-loving guts out a dozen times a day? The right to help me waddle to the bathroom and back later? To learn how to Lamaze breathe with me? The right to change shitty diapers and do midnight feeding duty? The right to buy the kid a car? Pay for college?"

She sensed how unreasonable she sounded but had completely lost the ability to be logical, or polite, or give a shit what they thought anymore. The past year and a half of her life had been such a turmoil, she felt buffeted by it, sore from it, and it had to stop. She was the only one with the ability to do that—to end the madness, the competition, their ongoing, never-ceasing need to fight over her, win her, whatever. Some women might be flattered but the hard reality of it, considering how different the two men where and how strongly she felt about at least one of them, was not fun or sexy or flattering. It was shitty.

Jack took a step towards her but she held out her hand, and he kept his distance. She kept her voice steady despite how shaky she was inside. Despite how hard she had to keep a grip on herself to not fall into Jack's suited arms and let him handle everything for her.

"I am doing this on my own. I'm giving you notice so when I get huge in the coming weeks you don't panic. Or get territorial. This is my baby. The end." She turned from them, gripped the edge of the kitchen counter. "You can go now." In her head, she begged one of them to stay.

The sound of the slamming door made her wince.

As was typical of many Michigan winters, this one seemingly had no end. By the time Ann Arbor hit mid-March people were cautiously optimistic. But St. Patrick's Day dawned cold, gray and threatening snow. Sara sighed and sat on the side of her bed, marveling at the glorious lack of nausea she'd been experiencing for a few weeks. She ran her hand over the hard lump that had appeared under her shirt, tucked the whole mess in the back of her brain, and focused on the busy day ahead.

Jack was considering taking the job as general manger of the Stewart Realty Company and had become distant and moody. That suited Sara fine and kept her from the temptation to let him back into her life. But that morning she had a meeting with him—one he'd called with a bunch of agents. For the first time in weeks, she wanted to go work. The crazed hormones roiling through her system were going to let her pretend she was normal again.

By the time she'd made it to her downtown office, snow was falling. Pretty. But not in March. She stomped her feet at the back door, smiling when Craig poked his head out of his cubicle.

"Hi," she said.

"Hi, yourself." He ambled over to her, his dark eyes taking her in from head to toe. "You look like a million bucks. Got a closing?" She brushed the dampness from her hair.

"No, a meeting at admin. But thanks. I feel pretty good for a change. A minor miracle." She grabbed a coffee cup, remembered her vow to cut back on the caffeine and filled it with water instead. A strange energy surged through her making her anxious and unable to settle. It was like she had reverted to her old self. The before preggers Sara she wished like hell she had back most days.

How could you get anyway? Knocked up. Jesus. How lame. It was the twenty-first century. You are a modern, independent woman. No one forced you to not use a condom.

She really had no excuse.

She stood, then dropped back into her chair, her mouth hanging open.

"Oh my God."

Craig barreled into the break room.

"What," he demanded, his voice low. "Are you okay?" His dark eyes flitted over her body a minute, then back up to her face. She gaped at him, not sure it had actually happened. Then she felt it again. A bizarre, fluttery sensation inside her. Like an eyelash, swiping against the inside of her stomach. An impossible feeling to describe but one she immediately identified.

"Wow." She put her hand on the hard bump under her shirt. It seemed to have shifted, changed shape. She stared at Craig.

"Seriously Sara, you're freaking me out. What is it?" He pulled a chair up to hers. "Do you need to throw up? What? Talk to me."

The fear on his face made her giggle. Then as the laughter took hold she snorted, guffawed, did the proverbial laugh out loud, so loud a few of their colleagues glanced over the short divider at them.

Finally, she calmed, hiccupped, and took his hand, pressing it to her stomach. The butterfly wing fluttered again. Craig's eyes widened. "Wow." He stared at his hand, then at her. "I want to kiss you so much right now." His voice stayed soft and low.

They stared at each other for a full twenty seconds in silence. "No, thank you," she whispered. She wouldn't do that to him. Because Craig wasn't the man she wanted kissing her. She was determined not to fall back into tempting scripts with him—where she let him take care of her for the wrong reasons.

The satisfaction she felt for saying that that flooded through her for a brief moment, then quickly got hijacked by remorse. She put a hand to his face.

"I'm glad you got to share that with me," she said, then stood and made her way out into the main office. If she stayed, she wasn't sure what she'd do.

Being with either of the men in question was not in her plan.
Not anymore.

She'd proven herself to be a shitty girlfriend much less a wife. Her temper got the best of her too much. She had too much trouble trusting anyone. She'd only make either of their lives miserable.

Jack had figured it out and was leaving her alone, after all.

Which is why she'd decided to focus on herself. And her baby.

Chapter Two

• • • •

"I'M A LITTLE WORRIED about your blood pressure." The doctor frowned at her handheld computer screen. Sara sat on the hard, too-small examination table. Her legs felt heavy, weighed down, and had for the last several days. Her mouth was constantly dry and at times, after the slightest exertion, her heartbeat would pound in her ears, making her dizzy. Ridiculous, considering her high level of fitness. She should have a flawless pregnancy. The concept that she'd screw this most basic of female jobs made her insane with worry and self-doubt.

"I'm fine."

"No, actually, you aren't. I'm going to have to report this to your dad. You came in here spotting, remember?"

"Oh please, Lisa, don't." She stared at the woman who'd been such a great help to her so far, who'd come with her father's professional blessing. She'd not been his first choice of obstetricians – which was one of the reasons Sara had chosen her from the list her father, the former head of obstetrics at the University hospital, had given her. She sat up, too fast it seemed.

"Whoa." She blinked, as the room got bright, then dimmed. "Damn." Lisa eased her back onto the table.

"That's it. I'm admitting you. I'm not worried about the baby, really. Getting a strong heartbeat there. But you're spilling proteins in your urine and..."

Sara closed her eyes and tried to ignore how fast and loud her own heartbeat sounded. Nausea hovered on her horizon. "Ugh."

Lisa patted her leg.

"I'm calling your dad now, under threat of death. I won't cross Dr. Matthew Thornton, Sara, sorry. I don't like the look of your BP, the edema in your legs, none of it. Who can you call to bring your stuff to the hospital?"

"You mean I can't go home first?" Panic hovered, but that made her face sweaty, which didn't help the whole pounding heartbeat thing. She took a breath.

"No. Ambulance is on its way."

"Ambulance! Isn't that a bit reactionary?" Sara tried to sit, but the room spun. "Okay, never mind."

"Who am I calling for you Sara? Blake?"

Sara tried to focus on the ceiling to keep from puking. Fear and a lick of anger erupted in her chest. She refused to be some kind of invalid pregnant lady. She gritted her teeth. "No. Call Jack." She'd provided the requisite list of emergency phone numbers, including, in order, her brother, Jack, Craig, her parents, Rob.

"Okay then." Lisa patted her leg and turned to the phone. A weird blanket of exhaustion seemed to smother her. "Don't go to sleep," Her doctor demanded, pinching her toe.

"Ow, dammit! I thought pregnant ladies got to sleep a lot."

"Not until I get you over to the U of M. I want monitors on you first. So stay with me, okay?" Sara nodded, but keeping her eyes opened proved harder than she imagined.

By the time she awoke she was hooked up to an IV, and Jack stood at her bedside, giving the attending doc the third degree. His voice soothed her like no other. She smiled and drifted off again, content that he had it all in hand.

Her dreams were a random, crazy mess of images. When she forced herself awake she was eyeball-to-eyeball with her father. He was glaring at her, but her mother elbowed him in the ribs so he finally smiled and put down the tablet computer he'd been clutching.

"God, Mom, how long was I out?" Sara stretched, and was more relieved than she cared to admit at the energetic fluttering under her hospital gown. Thank God she hadn't totally messed this up and lost the baby.

"So, young lady, looks like you get take a little vacation."

"Dad, being pregnant is not a vacation. I sincerely hope you never used that lame line with your patients." Her mother fussed around with her blankets, her lips twisting as she tried not to laugh.

"Well, um, anyway..." He harrumphed some more, glared at what Sara assumed was her record on the small screen. "You have to stay off your feet for at least another week. Completely off your feet. Do you comprehend what that means?"

"I think so, yeah. You did pay for four years of college. I'm not an imbecile."

"Sara," her mother muttered, patting her shoulder. Sara shrugged her off, suddenly so angry she could spit nails.

"When can I get out of here?" She slumped back on the pillows, feeling like a pissy adolescent, which made her even madder. "I'm hungry." A nurse bustled in, followed by a trailing cloud of young doctors. They spent about twenty minutes being awestruck by her father's August presence, made suggestions about her condition and treatment and left. "Can I not be a guinea pig please?"

"This is a teaching hospital, Sara. Deal with it." They glared at each other a minute before his phone buzzed. He turned away to answer it.

"I'll get some food. What're you hungry for?" her mother asked, still hovering.

"The hottest Mexican food on the planet." She bit back the urge to tell her mother to call Jack, have him bring it over. "Where did Jack go? He was here wasn't he?"

"Yes, he was. He was obviously uncomfortable though so I sent him home."

"Uncomfortable?" Sara let a small finger of irritation tickle the back of her brain. Who was really more uncomfortable, for crying out loud?

"He was as pale as a ghost. Told me he had a 'thing' about hospitals. Nothing logical, like most phobias. But he did a lovely job handling things until Blake got here. We drove down from Traverse as soon as we heard." She patted Sara's foot under the thin blanket. "Craig was here too, for a bit. Then he had to go."

"Hey!" Blake poked his head around the door. Sara's face brightened at the sight of him. "Look what I found on the way in." He held up a greasy bag. Sara's mouth watered.

"You read my mind, brother."

"One of my many parlor tricks. Here, eat this crap before I toss it in the incinerator. My car smells like a taco truck. Disgusting."

Chapter Three

"What do you mean, you can't make it?" Sara struggled to heave herself out of the car and onto the too-hot asphalt. She glanced at her watch. Late for Lamaze again. She sighed, anticipating the long-suffering sighs of the crunchy granola woman who led the class.

Her brother croaked in her ear. "I'm sick as a dog, Sara. I gotta sleep. Doctors put me on antibiotics for Strep. I can't do the Lamaze thing today. Sorry."

She repressed the need to yell at him.

Don't be selfish. The entire world doesn't revolve around your sorry pregnant ass.

"Okay. Take care of yourself. Is Rob there?"

"He will be in about an hour."

She sighed, made more "take care of yourself" noises and hung up, leaning on the warm metal of her car, trying to catch her breath. Who would have thought she'd be one of those fragile pregnant ladies? She hated every breathless, worrying, feet-up moment of it. Her phone buzzed.

Jack.

She smiled and answered it. "Where are you right now?"

"Headed home from a closing. Why? What do you need?"

Sara settled down on the floor, which was no mean feat, and smothered a grin when Jack appeared. He stuck out like a be-suited sore thumb, but she loved the sight of him. He was yammering into his phone as he walked, his deep laughter bouncing through the room, drawing yet more attention to him. The class leader strode over and held out her hand. He stared at it.

"I'll have to call you back," he said before ending the call. The woman kept her hand outstretched, a serene smile on her face. "Um, hello." He shook her hand. The class tittered.

"This is a device-free zone, if you please. The radiation is a known carcinogen. Do you want your child subjected to that in the womb?" He frowned down at his dangerous device.

"I'll keep it in my pocket." He saw Sara and started towards her.

The woman side stepped with him, crossed her arms and tapped her Birkenstocks on the soft, yoga-matted floor. "No, you won't. Give it to me. I keep them in another room."

"But..." Sara shot him a look. He handed it over. By the time he made it to her side, his face was red. "Hippies," he mouthed to her.

He smiled at a few people in the room. "I sold that guy his first house. But he wasn't with her then," he whispered. He raised a hand to another couple. "Those people are breeding? God help the human race." His low mutter near her ear made her more comfortable that she should be.

She elbowed him in the ribs. He sighed, shrugged out of his grey suit coat and expensive shoes and sat next to her. The next hour they giggled their way through the day's discussion: "Opening your vagina with your mind and positive energy."

"Hey, I can open vaginas with my...," he whispered.

"Shut up!" Sara elbowed him again and tried not to let the giggles overwhelm her. He leaned into her ear as the class leader seemed to go into some weird, trance-like state, extolling the virtues of olive oil on one's "pudendum" during the "stretching" process.

"Yum." He bit her earlobe, making her shiver.

"Yeah, I'll look like Jabba the Hut and smell like a plate of pasta."

He chuckled and stayed near her neck about a half-second too long. She turned and looked at him, flinching when he raised a hand and tucked a strand of hair behind her ear. "You are a gorgeous Jabba the Hut. I've missed you."

The teacher's voice broke the moment. "Now papas, please let the mamas settle in between your legs."

"What the...?" Jack looked away from her. Sara slapped his socked foot.

"Spread 'em." He grinned, and she maneuvered herself between his legs.

"Now, papas, touch your child." Sara winced. So many times she wished she could take back her words. Have the paternity test and let Jack claim the child in her belly. Because something in her knew it was his. "Like this." The Lamaze lady walked over, grabbed his hands, and put them on Sara's round stomach, moving them in circles for him. "Love mama's skin. Let your baby know you're there."

Jack's strokes were perfunctory at first. Sara sensed his uneasiness like a physical presence between them. Then she felt it—a bump, some pressure, then a distinct heel or elbow as the baby rolled and mounded on one side of her. "Holy shit," he blurted out. Sara blushed.

"Shhh..." the couple next to them admonished.

"Sorry." He leaned up, pressing his strong, warm torso against her back.

"Now, mama, lean back against him, let yourself relax. Inhale deep and clean. Let it out slow." The woman wandered off.

Sara closed her eyes. There was a crystal-clear rightness to this moment, sitting cradled between Jack's legs, his firm hands caressing her stomach as the baby seemed to sense a new presence and played hell with Sara's internal organs. She breathed deep.

"Relax," he whispered. "You're as tense as a damn guitar string. You heard the scary hippie lady. Breathe, already."

His deep voice conjured up memories and forced her into an odd, almost dreamlike, state. She let go of the near constant tension. "That's it, baby. Like that." His voice dropped an octave, and another sensation shot through her. A bolt of pure, unbridled horny made her shiver.

She shifted, kept her eyes closed, but her breathing got faster. His hands kept moving. The baby fluttered and then settled.

He rubbed and caressed all around the tight drum of her stomach. One hand made its way low, under the overhang of her belly. He growled in her ear. "I have such a hard on right now. Don't get up too fast." She grinned at his low-voiced admission.

"Mm hm." She pressed back against him as a sharp shaft of need pierced her brain. "You're gonna have to take me home after this." She kept her voice soft.

"Yeah. Well. Not happening. Friends, remember? You're doing this on your own and all that."

She heaved a sigh.

Your bed, Sara. Lie in it and stop being selfish.

"But seriously, don't move yet. I love the feel of you against me."

She let him soothe her for a few more minutes. When the Lamaze lady made them stand, Sara had to giggle at Jack's attempt to adjust himself. The sight of him, of what she knew damn well lay beneath that straining dress pants zipper, made her breathless. She turned away, angry at herself for making him do this, for putting them both through this face of "mommy, daddy, and baby" in this room full of earnest almost-parents.

"Now let's do our best middle school slow dance, shall we?"

Jack rolled his eyes but tugged her close. She put her arms around his neck, going up on her tiptoes to reach him, and whispered. "Thanks for coming with me."

"Sure. When's the next one?" She grinned, and gave him a light kiss, reveling for a half second in his familiar sensation of his lips.

Let him help you, be a friend, but that is it. That was your call. Stick by it.

"Next week." He pressed a hand into the small of her back, somehow providing just enough pressure to relieve the twinge of pain she'd developed sitting for so long.

"I'll be here."

Chapter Four

Craig stretched his legs and leaned back in the stiff office chair. He still had hours of work to do, but the bright sunshine streaming in the front office window distracted him.

He glanced at his phone and suppressed a frown of frustration. Suzanne had avoided agreeing to a date for weeks now, resisting him, making excuses, leaving town on random "beer research trips." He'd called her out on it during one of their late-night conversations and she'd admitted that she'd be around and not busy Friday. Tonight. And he was determined to make it a date worth remembering for them both.

Sara buzzed him with a text. The sight of her name did its usual number on his emotions. Guilt for having manhandled her last fall. Anger at her stubbornness over the paternity test issue. And the sick puppy-like thrill he always got thinking of her. Giving himself a mental shake, he picked up the phone and saw a text from Sara.

"Hey, I need some help. Just trying to get the last of the kitchen packed up."

"Where's Gordon?" He winced as he hit send, realizing how that sounded.

An email dinged into his inbox from Suzanne. His scalp tingled. Her go-slow approach, insisting they get to know each other as friends first before doing any more than the odd stolen kiss—it was about to kill him. But he looked forward to the sound of her voice more than anything.

"You said you were around, remember? Never mind."

He sighed and hit "call" next to her name.

"I'm sorry." He ran a hand through his hair. He'd been saying that a lot to her. It was getting old.

"It's fine. Short notice and it's a beautiful Friday afternoon. Why would you stand around in my chaotic kitchen and help me pack?"

"I can come by in the next hour. But I, um, I'm busy later."

Why he couldn't just say, "I have a date. With a woman I think I love" to Sara? The woman he believed he'd loved, once upon a time.

"Oh? Suzanne?"

He blew out a breath. "Yeah."

"Okay. That's good. Now that I can picture her as someone other than the woman who almost killed my brother back in the day, I approve."

He bit back the smart-ass comment about not requiring her approval. Their whole relationship entanglements in this group were hard to understand sometimes. And Sara's relationship with the woman he had developed a serious crush on was not his responsibility. "So, do you still need my help?"

"No, I think I'll go for a walk instead. I'm getting stir crazy in here."

He heard her sigh, and guilt flooded his brain again. "Sorry."

"Oh, stop being sorry. I'm fine. Have fun tonight, I mean it. I love the thought of you—happy. You deserve it."

"Yeah. Maybe." He stood, needing to end the conversation before he talked himself out of taking Suzanne out altogether. How he'd managed to find someone new amid all this crazy fucked up mess with Sara he couldn't imagine. But the thought of Suzanne's auburn hair, cut short, like a pixie cap, perfect for her petite frame, emphasizing her huge expressive eyes made a low buzz thrum through his brain. "Call me if you need me, Sara. I mean it. I'm not trying to be distant. You just caught me..."

She cut him off. "Trying to have a life. I'm the sorry one, Craig. I'm such a selfish cow sometimes. I realize that, believe me."

"Part and parcel of your mysterious and infinite charm." He grabbed his Ray-Bans and helmet and headed out into the warm afternoon. "Call me if you need anything and don't do stupid shit like whatever it is pregnant ladies do to bring on early labor. You aren't on bed rest anymore, I take it."

She laughed, and the sound warmed him, but in a way different than it used to. "No, I'm free to move about the cabin. Have fun and tell Suzanne I said hello."

"So, what's your major?" Craig lifted his beer and clinked glasses with his date. She smiled—a slow-moving, lovely thing that made his face burn hot. He hid his grin by taking a gulp of the beer she'd brought.

He'd made reservations at a good restaurant, but she'd called and insisted on bringing dinner over herself. Had a new beer she wanted to try out on him. So he'd showered, cleaned his long-neglected condo and tried to relax, playing his guitar for a while, then a video game.

He ended up in the bedroom, needing to relieve some of the pressure he'd been building up over the course of the last weeks. For a change, the face and lips he pictured on his at the last minute, sending him over the orgasmic edge, were not Sara's, but Suzanne's.

When she opened the door, juggling a couple of growlers and a huge container of pasta, he'd laughed and taken the growlers. They set up a picnic out on his balcony. His hands itched to touch her, but she exuded a big-time hands-off vibe today. So he decided to enjoy her company and some light conversation.

"Chemistry. I went to med school." Craig raised an eyebrow. "I'm full of surprises." She seemed distant, distracted.

"No doubt." He sipped more. "I bless this amazing IPA with my official approval, by the way. But it's big, isn't it?"

"Yeah, ten percent." She put her glass down and stared at him. He looked over his shoulder, making her laugh. "What's this about, anyway?"

"Uh, beer. I think."

"No, this." She made a little circling motion with her finger, encompassing them both. "Because I'm not sure I can..."

"Hold on, right there." Craig leaned back in his chair, hoping to put her at ease. "You're the one who wanted an intimate dinner at my place. I was gonna take you to Taco Bell or someplace equally romantic."

"Huh, funny enough, Taco Bell is my not-so-secret hidden vice, so there." She smiled. Craig decided silence was the better part of valor at that moment, so he ate and drank. And watched her. She rose after a few minutes, and stood next to him, her hand on his shoulder. He tried not to react, but lost the battle.

"Craig," she whispered as he stood in one smooth motion and pulled her in, covering her lips with his.

His phone buzzed. He ignored it as she pulled him back into his living room, onto the couch, and started fumbling with his zipper. He yanked her shirt off, gazed at the petite perfection of her breasts before cupping one and taking a pert pink nipple between his lips. She groaned, arched into him, threading her fingers in his hair.

"Yes," she whispered. "Please." His cock got even harder at the sound of her soft exhalations in his ear. He kissed her again, then eased her jeans down her slim hips.

"I like your philosophy about underwear." He nibbled her ear. "Sexy and yet, convenient."

"Shut up and kiss me some more." He did, drowning in her, trying to hold back the urge to take her, to make his mark on her. He'd never felt this way before, not even with Sara. Their whole sex life had been one long denial and argument, it seemed. But now, in his arms, was a woman who wanted him as much as he wanted her.

The damn phone buzzed again.

He groaned and tried to ignore it. "Craig," she gasped as he cupped one breast.

"Hmm?" He licked his way down her neck, nipped at each nipple, then moved lower as she squirmed and sighed.

"You should answer that."

He looked up from his southward journey. The reality of her lust swirled in his head, blinding him to anything and everything but Suzanne. She smelled of cinnamon somehow, or something else bright and spicy. He sighed and leaned across her to grab the infernal thing from the floor, where it had slipped from his pocket.

"Yeah?" He barked into it, groaning as Suzanne ran her bare foot over his lap.

"Craig?" a familiar male voice filled his brain.

Shit.

"What's wrong? Where is she?"

"University Emergency. Can you get there? I'm with my sister and her kids, but am leaving now," Jack said. "I'll be there in an hour."

Craig was already tugging his jeans back on. "What happened?"

"Not sure. They called me first. I called you and I'll get Blake next. Sorry."

"It's okay." He sat and dragged a shaking hand down his face. "I'm on my way. Don't leave there until I call you. It may be nothing."

He hung up and sighed.

"Sara?" Suzanne's voice had an edge to it he heard loud and clear.

"Yeah."

She sat up and grabbed her shirt. "Want me to come with you?"

"No, it's okay. Stay here, why don't you? I'd like to pick up where we left off."

Suzanne smiled, pulled him to his feet, and laid a tongue-tangling kiss on him. He held her close, trying to imprint himself on her. But she slipped out of his arms, grabbed her purse and started for the door.

"God damn it," he muttered, found his keys and followed her down to the parking garage. They didn't speak or touch.

"Someday," she said to him as she got into her car. "You'll understand that it's Jack, not you." Craig frowned at her.

"I already know that, Suzanne. Trust me." He bit back anything more lest he sound like an asshole, fired up the bike and roared out onto the downtown street. His head and body buzzed with missed opportunity and bad timing. Story of his fucking life.

Chapter Five

Jack jumped out of the car in front of Sara's condo, gave a quick knock, then opened the door. Floor-to-ceiling boxes and loud rock music assaulted his senses. He wandered into the kitchen and found her sitting at the table, staring into the middle distance. He snapped his fingers in front of her face.

"Your feast, Madame." He dropped the bananas, chocolate ice cream, and a can of lemonade on the table. He'd been stopping by every night for the last couple of weeks, bringing her the snacks she craved she could actually have—potato chips, jalapeños, and iced coffee being the forbidden ones thanks to their salt content or heartburn inducing qualities.

She glanced up at him, then down at the food. "Thanks." Her voice sounded thin. He put a hand on her shoulder.

"You okay?"

"Sure, just out of breath. You'd think I hadn't spent the last twenty years working out every single damn day. Ugh." She still had a bunch of silverware clutched in her hand. He pried them out of her grip and put them in the nearest open box. She sighed and placed her feet up in the chair.

"No more climbing ladders. You promised," he admonished her as he folded the stepladder. "Not after last month's adventure."

Sara put her head on her arms. "Poor Craig." Jack laughed. His friend Suzanne had ripped him a new one over that a few nights later as he sat at her bar.

"Can you keep your baby-mama out of my new boyfriend's life please, Gordon?"

The concept of his firebrand friend with the smooth Mr. Robinson made him smile every time he contemplated it—for more reasons than one.

"She could be your boyfriend's baby-mama," he'd reminded her and had narrowly missed getting brained by a flying beer mug. He'd helped her clean up the mess against the bar wall and they'd gotten buzzed together, like old times, but with a whole different set of problems and complications.

"I really, really like him," she'd said, leaning on his arm. He'd kissed the top of her hair.

"And I'm sure he feels the same way. He'd be insane not to. You deserve it, peaches." And she did. She'd had a hell of a ride with that asshole of an ex-husband. Then, rushing in with Blake after that had almost torn her apart, especially when she'd ended it. He'd made a mental note to talk to Craig and give him a heads up about what had happened.

Now, it seemed, he had Sara to himself once again. But for her damnable desire to keep him as "My Good Friend and Lamaze Buddy, Jack." To distract himself, he taped up a few boxes, labeled them, then found a beer in her fridge. He leaned against the counter and gazed at her.

It had taken him a solid three months to work his way back into her life. The time and energy she spent ignoring him and Craig as her pregnancy progressed after that first shocking conversation was admirable. But he'd worn her down.

Given the medical crises she kept having, she had no choice but to rely on them. By the time her parents had moved back to town and installed themselves in her life, he'd almost given up. However, a late night call from her brother convinced him otherwise. Blake was a surprising ally to be sure, but Jack would take it.

And then there were those Lamaze classes. He grinned at the sight of her now, lush, full, and ripe. His balls ached from lack of use, but he'd made a vow to himself. One he planned to keep.

"You're gorgeous, but you already know that."

She lifted her shirt, making him breathless with a weird possessiveness tinged with lust. "Really? Then what is that?" She pointed to a dark line that had appeared beneath her navel running down to her...

"Put your shirt down," he insisted.

"I mean, look at it."

Sighing, he stuffed a few towels on top of the last box of kitchen stuff and turned to face her. "No, Sara. I can't. It makes me want to do things to you, and you've already given me that ultimatum."

She groaned and toyed with the banana on the table. "I'm sorry. It's just..."

"I get it. I can be your friend. Can help keep you in lemonade and bananas, but that's it. Even if that is my kid in there." He sat across from her and cupped her chin.

"I didn't want this." Her voice cracked. "I am such a selfish, whiney bitch but this." She put a hand on the shelf of her almost nine-month pregnant belly. "This was not part of my plan."

"Yeah, life. It has a way of fucking up plans. And you are a whiny bitch. But I'll forgive you, since you're admitting it. It's the first step toward recovery, after all."

He stood, pulling her up with him, unable to resist, needing to comfort, to reassure, anything to stop the pain that had settled in his chest when he realized she was serious about keeping him at arm's length. He held her and let her cry herself out against his neck, ruining yet another crisp shirt collar. Running his hands up and down her back, loving the hard press of the baby between them, he whispered, murmured and cajoled her out of her funk.

He shut his eyes, sucking in deep breaths of her scent.

"What are you thinking right now," she mumbled as her arms crept around his neck.

"That I'd pay you for a kiss."

She laughed and stepped out of his embrace, leaving him cold. "Why? Haven't you done enough already?" Her smart-ass tone only made him want her more.

"Well hell Sara, according to you I'll never know that now will I?" He took her hand, pulled her to him again, sighing with contentment when their lips met. He held her close, or as close as her belly allowed. He took advantage of the moment to cup her full breast, run a hand over and around the ripe mound of her body. A sudden poke under his hand made him gasp and step back.

"Yeah, welcome to my world, Gordon." The moment gone, she flopped back in the chair. "You've had your grope. Now rub my feet."

"Bossy and bitchy. You are quite the charmer." But he welcomed any opportunity to have his hands on her skin. He dropped into the chair across from her, dug his knuckle into her instep, and attempted to ignore the hardening under his zipper at the sight of her sleek bare legs, and the way she leaned her head back and moaned. "Of course you realize this is the longest I've gone without sex in… ever." He cleared his throat, shifted in his seat, and put her foot back on the floor.

She glared at him, then her face softened. "Poor baby. Forgive me for not having more sympathy for your plight."

Letting his body lead, he got on his knees and parted her legs. A pure shaft of lust pierced his spine, nestled in for the long haul deep in his brain. He ran his hands up her thighs, over the tight skin of her stomach, marveling at the way her body had shifted and changed to accommodate life. Her fingers threaded in his hair as he kissed his way up her belly, lapped at her reddened nipples. By the time he reached her mouth, he was about to come in his pants.

"God, I miss you," he said around her lips.

"Shh, no talking," she insisted. "More kissing."

"Don't have to tell me twice." He pulled her back up, his head spinning, spine thrumming with energy.

Mine.

He put a hand on her stomach, loving the heat of her skin. "God, Sara," Jack groaned as she unzipped his jeans. "Why won't you let me...?"

She covered his mouth, shutting out words. His entire world narrowed, focusing again on his need for her. But he finished in his head: Why won't you let me be with you, all the time, take care of you every day? Why won't you let go of your infernal need to prove something by doing all of this alone?

She whispered in his ear. "Do you know the most comfortable position for me right now? Even just standing around?" He shook his head, ran his tongue down the line of her neck, tasting the newness of her. "Watch." She shrugged out of his arms and turned, propped her elbows on the bare kitchen counter, back arched, ass in the air.

"Dear Lord, woman." He exhaled, admiring the view. "I don't want to hurt you, but..."

"Please, Jack. I need it. I need... you."

Running both hands along her hips, he wrestled around and found his better self, and dragged that bastard out to the light of day.

"No. I'm not playing man-shaped dildo for you." His eyes burned at the sight of her beautiful ass. He bit down on the need to slip inside her. She spread her legs wider. "I can't be your fuck buddy, baby. I won't. I'm too invested." He sighed and pulled her shorts back up, using the opportunity of proximity to caress the heavy swell of her stomach.

She squirmed, wiggled her ass against him. "No fair," he muttered into her hair.

She made a whimpering noise and turned around to face him. Tears stood in her eyes. Without thinking, he reached out, wiped them away, and kissed her again. She broke away. "Stop. You're right. I'm not being fair."

He sighed, ran his fingers through his hair, and willed his libido back in its cage. It went, but with a warning growl that did not bode well for his mood later.

"So, you closed last week. You move this week, right?" He propped his hands on the counter behind him, opposite her, keeping his distance. She sighed and put a hand on the small of her back.

"Yeah. Then the whole baby comes out part I've read about but... oh hell." She waddled out into the living room.

"My offer is still on the table." He waited. She stuck her head back into the room.

"And my answer is still no. Unless it's a new offer to help me paint the baby's room."

"Do you realize you've now refused an offer that countless women have cast themselves into the sea over, not once, but three times? And I hate painting. Hire somebody."

She stuck her tongue out at him.

"Goes to show those women were weak. I'm stronger and can resist your charms. As for painting, it only means something if you do it yourself."

"You're the most stubborn female on God's green earth. I don't know why I hang out with you. I'm gonna go. I'll email you the numbers of my favorite painting crew."

"Better, before I take advantage of you in a way you'll enjoy."

He grinned. "Promises, promises." Unable to stop himself, he put his hand alongside her cheek.

She sighed and leaned into his palm, making the already unbearable band around his chest tighten further.

"You're killing me and here I go, asking again." He took a deep breath. "Marry me Sara. Let me take care of you and the baby." He ran his hand over her belly again. "Stop fighting it, why don't you? What the hell are you trying to prove?"

She stepped back and crossed her arms. "That I can be an adult on my own, that's what. I did this. I'm the one who should've required condoms. That was my responsibility, but I didn't take it."

Again, unable to stop himself, frustrated by her damnable independent streak, he pulled her close and pressed his nose into her hair, relishing all the memories of her, of them, good and bad. Sure, the whole insta-family thing wasn't something he'd bargained for. The longer she held him off, the more he wanted her. Feeling weak, but with an onrushing sensation of anger at her, all of it, all at once. His usual response to Sara. No, he wasn't perfect. She was right to be wary. His temper got the best of him too much. He was a know-it-all—never mind that he knew a shit ton about a lot of shit. He understood her reticence.

But still… "I want to take care of you and the baby, Sara. There, I said it again. But I'm done begging you for anything. We clear?"

She shrugged out of his embrace. "Good. It's not a good look on you. Thanks for helping me and for the snack. See you tomorrow, I guess. Got an appointment in the morning. Hopefully, they'll give me a get-out-of-jail-free card. If I have to sit around here much longer…"

He put a finger over her lips. "Enough of that. Do what the docs say. Promise me." He kept his voice light.

"Whatever. I'm sick of being such a goddamned invalid."

"Yeah, so is the rest of Ann Arbor."

"Go away. Leave me alone to pout and feel sorry for myself."

He touched her nose, stuffed his hands in his pockets to keep from picking her up and dumping her in his car. The need to take care, to possess, to be hers, blinding him for a minute. He closed his eyes. When he reopened them, she had a funny look on her face.

"You okay, Jack?" The softness in her voice hit him right in the gut. Because he hadn't been exaggerating. He'd be her friend and Lamaze coach. But not more. He had to move on or he risked a stroke or heart attack, or worse.

"No. But that's your fault so…"

He left, while the word "mine" beat a constant, insistent pulse in his heart.

His phone dinged with a text as he was sitting at home, alone, bourbon in hand, pondering his options to purge Sara Thornton from his heart and head once and for all.

"Are you gonna help me paint the damn kid's room or what? I need to get it done this weekend."

He grinned like an idiot as he responded. "Well, if you're going to ask that nicely, I guess I can't refuse. I'll get the supplies. You order the color but do NOT ask me about it because that's one thing I refuse to decide."

Her reply came within seconds. "Thanks, Jack. I appreciate your help."

"You just want me around so you can stare at my ass."

"Oh dang. Busted. See you Saturday, say, 3 p.m.?"

"Your wish, oh Mighty Pregnant Queen. My command."

"That's more like it."

Chapter Six

"Sara! What are you doing here?" The sales secretary stood, alarm in her eyes. "I mean, it's good to see you, but..." Her voice trailed off as Sara heaved her awkward bulk through the front door. She sighed and dropped into one of the low slung chairs, half wondering how in the hell she'd be able to stand back up, but not really caring, as long as she could sit.

"If I stayed in that frigging oven of a house surrounded by boxes another minute, I was gonna... ouch." She put a hand on the huge swell of her stomach, pressing a heel or hand or something away from her ribs. "How in God's name does anyone think this is nice? I hate it." She shoved her hair out of her eyes.

Several of her colleagues entered the public space at the front of her downtown real estate sales office. She tried to focus on them, but she hurt all over, and there was a pounding in her head that she knew damn good and well didn't bode well for her blood pressure.

She'd been so stir crazy at home alone, all she'd wanted to do was move around, even if it meant going out into the ungodly August heat. Her phone buzzed, and she dug it out, groaning at the sight of her father's number—again.

"Hi Dad." She shifted her feet up onto the coffee table, hoping that would help ease the swelling in her ankles. Pam took a seat next to her, pointing and frowning at her feet. "No, I'm taking it easy, like you said."

Her father rattled off more statistics, asked for the millionth time why she wouldn't get a paternity test now that the baby was almost thirty-seven weeks, then berated her a while longer. She listened, adding "uh-huh's" and "sure's" and a few "spare me's," ignoring most of it and wishing once again that he was not a retired obstetrician.

"Dad, just because you know everything that can go wrong doesn't mean..." He cut her off with more facts about her condition.

Sara stopped listening. It wasn't like she hadn't lived through it—the bed rest within ten weeks for a misplaced placenta or some shit. The gross, high-protein diet for the next trimester thanks to all the weight she lost throwing up morning, noon and night for the first three months. Now, swelling, headaches, high-blood pressure and the usual fun of having to pee every ten minutes, which made getting any significant sleep impossible.

"Dad, the doctor said I was close enough to term that if I went into labor now." She paused. "I had to get out of there, okay? I was going nuts!" She sighed. "Don't make me hang up on you again. Where's Mom? Let me talk to her."

The minute her doctor had called her father with news of early complications, her parents had moved back to Ann Arbor and into a condo. They'd been doing everything in their power to make her insane ever since. Between her father's busybody meddling with her appointments, and her mother's passive-aggressive micromanaging of everything else, it was no wonder her blood pressure shot up on a regular basis.

At her last emergency room visit, she'd been proud of her doctor, standing up to the Great and Powerful Doctor Thornton, letting Sara go home after doing all the ultrasounds and testing to make sure the baby was fine.

Then she'd fallen and landed hard on her ass after losing her balance on a low stepladder. No big deal. But after getting up and recovering her dignity, she'd noticed blood in her panties, had panicked and called 911. It was nothing. Just a late-term spotting thing, but her father had been apoplectic, again.

"We've been through this. I don't want him there." She held out a hand and her friend, Val, hauled her to her feet. Her back had developed a dull ache. She had a sudden urge to get up and move around.

Her skin crawled with tension at the sound of her father's voice now that the conversation had taken its usual turn in the "why isn't that asshole around more" direction. Trying to explain the complexity of her relationship with Jack to her father only made her more exhausted. So she didn't try. He'd form his own opinion anyway, regardless of what she told him.

She waddled out of the public space and down the hall towards the conference room. The air conditioning made her shiver as she slid into a leather chair at the head of the table.

"No, it's not the immaculate conception. Yes, I realize the baby has a father. No, I don't know who he is. Yes, it could be Jack. Okay Dad—now will you please stop harping?" She winced, trying not to let him hear her groan while readjusting herself in the seat. The sound of her heartbeat pounding in her ears was making her sweaty. "I'm gonna go. You're stressing me out. Yes, I love you too, bye."

She laid her head down, letting the cool granite surface soothe her overheated skin. After a few minutes, she figured she'd survive and stood.

A wave of dizziness coupled with a wallop of nausea forced her back. The baby rolled hard. "Ow." She put a hand on her stomach, suddenly scared. "Hey, um, is anybody out there?" A bright white bolt of pain slammed her between the eyes. She took a minute to think that the hippie Lamaze lady didn't say anything about headaches as part of child birth. Then her feet went numb, and the room dimmed. "Help?" She grabbed her phone, using a familiar number on reflex.

"You okay?" Jack's deep voice rumbled through her psyche, calming her just as her heart started pounding so badly it made her breathless. She looked down. A puddle had formed at her feet. Her legs were drenched. Her water must have broken.

"No," she whispered. "No. I'm not."

"Where are you?"

"Office. Ow! Shit!" A band tightened around her middle, clamping down on her lower back and abdomen with so much force it brought tears to her eyes.

"What? Why aren't you...? Never mind. Call 911. I'm around the corner. Be right there."

The phone slid from her hand, landing in the pool of fluid on the floor. She squinted at it, realizing that it was red. That she was bleeding.

Holy shit.

A tidal wave of pain and nausea bowled her over. She couldn't get a breath. "I can't feel my hands." She stared at her fingers, wiggling them, amazed, in a haze of agony. "Help." She tried to stay conscious. Her last memory was of arms cradling her and the sound of a deep voice.

"Stay with me, Sara. I mean it. Somebody call a fucking ambulance already!"

"Jack?" she whispered as the room darkened to black.

Craig dismounted his bike, tucked the helmet under his arm, and stretched. Two late nights of studying plus three gigs that week had taken their toll. His whole body thrummed with fatigue. The sight of Sara's BMW in the lot made him frown. She was supposed to be home, off her feet.

The minute he stepped into the back office hallway, he sensed something wasn't right. He dropped his helmet on a desk and ran to the front, ignoring the strange emptiness of a busy summer real estate office. A sharp, coppery odor stung his nose, making his heart race.

As he turned the corner separating the conference room from the open office area, he heard it. A soft moan, then the slam of a door, then nothing. His ears buzzed and his stride lengthened, but the hall was like ten miles of empty road.

As he approached the large conference room door, he stopped, hearing only the sounds of his own breathing and laughter from the storefront side of the office. But he sensed her there, somewhere.

"Sara?" His throat closed up when the knob wouldn't cooperate, but he wrestled it open. His first thought upon entering was that someone had spilled red paint all over the carpet. Once his brain registered the scene, he saw her, half under the table, curled in a ball and moaning. "Dear Christ, Sara."

He sat down and tried to pull her into his lap. As he watched in helpless horror, her eyes rolled back, and her body stiffened in a terrifying seizure. "Stay with me, Sara. I mean it." He glanced up. Pam and Chris stood looking on in shock, phones in hand. "Somebody call a fucking ambulance!"

As Sara's body calmed, he brushed her hair back. No longer caring he sat in a pool of her blood. His ears roared, but he kept his voice soft. She opened her eyes.

"Jack?"

He smiled, kissed her nose, the cloying odor of blood and fear clogging his brain. "No honey. It's Craig. Try to relax. We've called an ambulance. Everything will be all right."

The next minutes passed like hours. Sara faded in and out of consciousness, and the ogling crowd grew larger.

"Oh God, it hurts...." Her loud moan ripped through his gut. When a hand touched his shoulder, he jerked away, trying to focus on her.

"Sir, please, let us handle this."

He let the paramedic pull Sara off his lap. "Are you hurt?" The woman's eyes traveled up and down him as her partner laid Sara back and started taking her vital signs. He looked down at the apparent carnage reflected on his clothes. Her blood. So much of it. He swallowed hard.

"No, no, it's not me. I found her here like this, sat down and...." His brain focused. "Take her to the UI. I'll meet you there."

"Okay dad, calm down. We need to get her stabilized first." The woman patted his arm. By now, the entire office had collected in the hallway, staring at the bloody scene. Craig struggled to comprehend what she'd said to him.

"I'm not…" He looked up as Jack Gordon came barreling through the door separating the public from the private part of their sales office. "I mean, is she okay? She seized on me for about fifteen seconds."

"Let's get her out of here." The medics bustled around without answering him. "Excuse me, sir, you need to move aside."

Jack stood, staring at the room, mouth agape, eyes wild. Craig took in what the man saw—the floor darkened with Sara's blood while her back arched and feet pounded against the carpet when another seizure gripped her.

Jack's face drained of color. "Sir!" The medic shoved Jack out of the way and rolled the gurney in. Once she stilled, the EMTs lifted her up and hustled her out into the waiting ambulance.

"You okay?" Craig narrowed his eyes at Jack.

"No, I'm not."

Jack turned, pushed his way through the gathered crowd and ran outside, demanding to be let into the ambulance with her. Craig grabbed his helmet and rushed out behind Jack. He followed the ambulance through midday streets, taking deep breaths to calm his heart, forcing himself to focus on the traffic while long forgotten prayers raced through his brain.

Jack watched from a safe distance as the emergency room staff hooked Sara up to machines and tubes, talking quietly while getting her stabilized. His brain refused to comprehend the scene. The sight of her body, swollen and continuing to stiffen with seizures, made him want to punch a hole in the wall. He closed his eyes, hoping to erase some of the trauma from his reality.

Why the fuck would she not listen to doctors? Her own father, for Christ's sake.

When he made the extreme mistake of opening them, a drip of bright red blood splashed to the floor beneath the bed where she was lying, which made his stomach do flips. He groaned and focused on not passing out.

A hand dropped onto his shoulder. Craig's dark eyes met his. The man's pants and half his shirt had stiffened. Dark with her blood. "We need you."

Jack frowned at him. "I don't do blood." But he got to his feet. Sara needed him.

"She's come to, but she's crying and won't relax. They can't get the needle in her spine."

Jack held up a hand and attempted to keep the room from spinning. "Please, I don't want any details." They both looked up at the sound of Dr. Matt Thornton's roar of outrage as he stomped into the curtained area.

"What the fuck do you think you're doing? Get her upstairs. You will not operate on my daughter in this filthy ED."

The commotion he caused made Jack's hackles rise. He followed Craig across the room, listening to the man berate and brow beat every doctor and nurse in a five-mile radius. Jack settled himself at Sara's head, focusing on her eyes, brushing away the tears that streamed down her chalk-white face. One of the guys moving around between her raised legs seemed to be in charge. He pointed at Jack, then at Craig and Matt.

"Who are all of you people? Can I get this space cleared out please? I have to perform an emergency C-section right now."

"The hell you will. I'm her father, former head of obstetrics at this hospital, and I want her upstairs in a sterile room," Dr. Thornton bellowed.

Jack looked at Sara and kept smoothing her hair back. She locked in on him. "Listen to me, Sara." He kept his voice low, adopting a low, neutral tone. "Relax. Roll up on your side. These guys are trying to help you." She groaned and closed her eyes.

"I can't. Make it stop, Jack. Please... oh God..." Her body tensed and she grabbed his arm.

"Sara, I mean it. Open your eyes and look at me." She did, and the pain he saw in them made his teeth ache. "Take a breath, keep your eyes on mine, and roll towards me. I won't let go of you, I promise."

As her father and the emergency doctor argued about seizure meds and placentas, Jack forced himself to stay calm, keep his eyes still, and fixed on hers. She winced, then rolled. He put a hand on her belly.

"That's it, baby. Relax. Let them do what they need to do." He frowned when she flinched and cried out, but kept up his stream of soothing noises. Craig nodded at him, letting him know whatever needed doing had been done. She stuck out a shaking hand, touched his face. He saw her fingers come away wet.

"All right, the lot of you, out of here, now. This is my patient, and there are too many people in my way." Jack swallowed hard, kissed her dry lips, and stood.

"No," she whispered, reaching out her arm. "Stay. Please."

"Sara." Her father's firm voice broke the moment. "Lie back. Let them get your baby out. He's not doing well. Do you understand, sweetheart? We have about three minutes to get him out or—"

Jack turned to the tall, imposing man who would as soon stab him through the heart with a rusty fork as acknowledge he might be the father of his grandchild. "I'm staying."

He surprised himself with that. He didn't do blood, or even emergencies that required medical professionals if he could avoid them. But he squared his shoulders and glared at Sara's father. Her loud groan made them both look down at her. Craig crouched down on her other side. She gripped his hand.

"I'm so tired." Her eyelids fluttered. "Can I sleep? Please?"

The attending doc nodded to a nurse, who pushed Craig aside. "No, Sara. Stay awake," the woman said as they draped the lower half of her body with blue paper. Jack held one hand and Craig the other.

Within a few minutes, there was a high, thin wail. Jack's scalp tingled as he looked up to see a small, slimy-looking, pink body pulled from the tented area around her stomach. At that split second, he almost forgot his lifelong phobia about hospitals.

"Sara?" The edge in Craig's voice startled him. He looked down in time to see her eyes close before the monitors in the room sent up a cacophony of noise. A team of scrub-suited people rushed in, shoving all of them aside. Sara's father started to talk, but Jack pulled him out of the way. The three of them stood watching, both of them helpless as the doctors revived her.

He leaned against the wall and slid to the floor just as Sara's mom came rushing down the hall. Finally, the beeping noises leveled off, and the team backed away. Her father rushed back toward the bed, but Jack stayed frozen, his gaze fixed on Sara's face as her eyes flickered open.

Craig stood by the table where a nurse fussed around with the baby. He watched as the man lifted a tiny blanket-wrapped bundle into his arms.

"It's a girl." Sara's mother knelt down and pressed her lips to Jack's cheek before he put his head on his hands and let tears slip down to the floor. "Both are fine, but Sara has to stay in the ICU until they get her stabilized. Go on, Jack. Get some air or some coffee or something." She pulled him up at the same moment Blake and Rob came rushing around the corner.

Jack marched straight to the bed, beating her brother by a couple of steps. Sara's eyes were half closed, but he touched her face and she blinked up at him. "I'm sorry," she whispered. "Such drama."

"That's you, babe. Always have to be the center of attention. Now get some rest. I'll be here."

Chapter Seven

Craig's arms shook, but when the baby opened her eyes and stared at him, he had never felt stronger in his life. She yawned, and her tiny features wrinkled as she let out a small cry.

Jack stayed parked by Sara's head, murmuring to her, brushing tears from her face. If Craig were a betting man, he'd lay even odds on the fact that Mr. Gordon had shed tears in the past few minutes. His whole body tensed when an alarm sounded near Sara's bed. A nurse rushed in, flipped a switch and stuck something in her IV.

Another nurse tapped him on shoulder, then took the baby from him.

"So, who beat me up with a Buick?" Sara's voice sounded scary weak.

Blake and Rob stood in the doorway. Blake had a hand clenched around Rob's arm but as soon as Sara saw him, she burst into tears, making alarms sound and a flurry of medical types rush in.

"All right you guys, let's give her some space, shall we?" A nurse eyeballed the collection of people in the room. "We're getting ready to move her up to ICU for observation. Only Dad stays with her, got it?" The woman seemed confused when Jack stood up.

"Ah, I'll stay," Blake declared. "These guys need a break." He pointed at Craig. "You need a shower and a change of clothes."

"And a drink," he said, noting the shaking in his hands. The whole scene had been wild, intense, and amazing. It had set his nerve endings ringing, but he didn't want to leave. He wanted to stay, watch, and listen to the doctors and nurses as they went about their daily business of saving lives.

When he looked up and saw Suzanne walking down the corridor, relief shot through him like an ice-cold splash of water. But the adrenaline rush whooshed out with it, leaving him dizzy.

"Better sit down before you fall down." She took his hand and drew him out to a chair in the hall. He caught a look between Blake and Rob at the sight of her, but was too exhausted to deal with it. He let her tug him down into a seat. "I hear you were quite the hero." Craig put his head in his hands, trying to quell the nausea that rose at the memory of Sara lying in all that blood. "C'mon, let me run you home."

He looked up at her, surprised, but not at all unhappy with the suggestion. For six weeks, he'd avoided her, embarrassed at how quickly he'd left her behind in favor of Sara's latest medical crisis. But the sight of her now made him want to weep with relief.

They both stood when an orderly rolled Sara's bed out, still attached to a bunch of monitors and IV lines. Blake walked alongside her, his hand clutched in hers. Jack slumped against the wall next to Craig, Suzanne, and Rob. Sara's parents followed behind her, Matt shooting eyeball daggers at Jack. Craig flinched when Suzanne put a hand on his leg.

"Let's go."

His chest tightened at the sight of the small clear plastic bassinet now rolling past them. He stood, put a hand on it to stop the nurse. "Wait. I..." He looked down at the now sleeping infant. "She's okay, right?" The nurse glanced at him, then at Jack, looking confused at all the possible dads in the room. The doctor who'd delivered the baby appeared around the corner and put a hand on Craig's shoulder.

"Yes, she is."

Jack shook the man's hand. "Thank you."

The doctor looked around at the men and shrugged. "It's my job. Now you should all get some rest. The baby fun has just begun. Trust me. I have twins at home." He clapped Jack on the back and started running down the hall to his next crisis. Craig stared after him.

"Does she have a name?" Suzanne asked as she stood and smiled at the group.

"Uh, don't know. Not yet, I don't guess." Craig tried not to collapse from residual stress.

"Kate," Jack said, as he sunk into the seat Craig had vacated. "Katherine Elizabeth." They all stared at him. "She picked it and a boy's name last week." Craig studied Jack's face. His heart felt frozen in ice, realizing what he had denied for the last months. "But me knowing that doesn't change anything." He stared straight at Craig. "So don't worry."

He stood and stretched, then stuck his hand out. Craig took it, wary but too shattered to think much about the gesture. "Thank you. You saved her life, both of their lives." He ran a hand over his face. "I'm a wreck. You handled everything well, very well." Craig put a hand on the other man's arm, but words escaped him.

He watched as Rob put an arm around Jack's shoulders. "This is about as fucked-up a celebration as it gets but, can I buy you a beer? Something harder?" The blonde man smiled at them both, let his eyes flick over the attractive redhead at his side. "Suzanne."

She lifted her chin. "Rob." Without thinking about it, Craig slipped his arm around her waist in a lame attempt to defray the tension. She shrugged him off. "I'm okay. Let's go." Rob raised an eyebrow at him before he turned, forcing his wobbly legs to move forward. He felt like he could sleep for a week.

By the time they pulled into his condo's underground parking garage, Craig realized something about the slight redheaded woman behind the wheel—she was not only one of the most attractive women he'd ever seen, but she had an aura of calm about her that took the tension right out of him.

"Coming up?" he asked, one hand on the door, not sure if he wanted it or not. His feelings for Sara and the baby he'd watched taken from her body represented the most complicated set of emotions he'd ever experienced. The past year had been a whirl of together, apart, together and apart—and then, the big news.

Suzanne smiled, and it lifted his heart, forcing words from his lips.

"I would like for you to, you know, come upstairs with me."

"All right." She followed him to the lift.

He slid his key card into the elevator's locking mechanism and punched his floor number. Once they entered his space, she wandered into the kitchen, leaving him to ponder the weird turn of events of the previous twelve hours.

He could be a father, then again, he might not be. He loved Sara in a sort of low-grade way. So much his head still pounded at the memory of her body seizing and the sounds of the beeping alarms around her. Then again, he sensed himself falling into something much more than mere infatuation with the woman rummaging around in his refrigerator.

Feeling like a side story in a daytime drama, he staggered into the bathroom. After shucking his shirt and pants and throwing them straight into the garbage, he turned the shower on full-blast hot. Letting steam spill into the room, he flopped down on his bed and tried to still his whirling emotions.

He launched himself off the bed when a hand landed on his bare chest. "What the..." His heart pounded in his ears. Suzanne stood, cup of coffee in hand, concern in her gaze. "Shit. How long did I sleep?" He reddened and tugged the duvet over his nakedness.

"Over an hour. I came in to check on you and turned off your shower before you drained the building of hot water." He groaned and flopped back onto the pillow. "I'm gonna go. You rest."

"No, no, wait. I'm usually not such a shitty host." Keeping the bed cover more or less wrapped around his waist, he side stepped into the bathroom and shut the door. "I'll make us something to eat. Give me a minute." He shuddered when the water hit his skin.

An hour later, stomachs full of omelets and strong coffee, they sat together on the couch, feet up on the coffee table, in companionable silence. After filling her in on his story, the dead father, abandoned college degree, he stopped and looked up at the ceiling for a minute.

"You know, I think I want to go to medical school. I almost have my bachelor's in chemistry, anyway. Why not?"

She stared at him. "Okay."

"I know, kind of a shock, but today was such a buzz..." To his surprise, she laid her head on his shoulder. After a minute, he put his arm around her.

"My late husband was a doctor."

"Oh. Small world. I mean, you know..."

"I know. Full of surprises. That's me." Craig sighed when she snuggled in closer. "I don't have a pretty story, Craig. I'll warn you now."

"Who does?"

She laughed, and when she lifted her face to his, kissing her seemed like the most perfect thing to do, ever.

Chapter Eight

Sara slapped at the alarm clock, but it wouldn't stop blaring. She sat and gasped at the pain that assaulted her every nerve ending.

Holy shit, even my hair hurts.

She looked up at the ceiling and tried to get her bearings. The sound kept going and, in some sick perversion of Pavlov's principle, her breasts tingled and started to leak. She groaned and rolled onto her stomach, remembering that her mom had left the day before after six long weeks of hovering. Damn if she wouldn't give anything for the woman to be back. If only to go pick the baby up now and placate her for a while so Sara could sleep a few more minutes.

The mewling progressed to crying. The pillow Sara pulled over her own head didn't shut it out. When the sound grew to a full-throated screech, Sara heaved herself out of bed and stumbled across the hall, tripping over the boxes still sitting half opened and ignored, figuring she'd stumbled into the eighth circle of hell.

By three o'clock that afternoon, convinced she had not a single mothering gene in her entire body, Sara sat on the couch, still in her pajamas, baby puke on one shoulder. Katie had cried so long and enthusiastically, she was reduced to pitiful hiccups interspersed with hoarse yelps before drifting off. As she'd quieted, the doorbell rang, making them both jump.

"Shit, shit, shit," Sara muttered as she placed the baby on a blanket on the couch and prayed to all that was holy for her to stay asleep for a few minutes before opening the door. She burst into tears at the sight of Craig, his crooked, familiar smile the best thing she'd seen in a week. Suzanne lurked behind him, holding a plate of homemade cookies.

Craig hugged her, then pushed her back, his nose wrinkling. "Yeah, I'm here. Go take a shower. You reek."

"With pleasure. She's over there. Good luck." Sara escaped to the upstairs of the small Cape Cod she'd purchased. Katie had been so easy for a few weeks, then all colicky hell had broken loose, just in time for Sara's parents to go back up to their house in Traverse City—mainly to keep Sara from killing her father, as his insufferable bossiness from her pregnancy lingered and then some into her life as mother of a newborn. But at that moment, Sara had never felt more abandoned in her life. She and Katie had sat and cried together for a solid hour that day. And things had devolved from there.

She'd even take her father's constant stream of advice if it meant her mother could come back and help her.

Reinforced but still bone tired after a hot shower, she emerged to the sound of actual cooing. She tugged on jeans and a t-shirt and made her slow way downstairs. Craig sat with Katie on his legs, which he had bent up, his feet propped on a small, un-opened cardboard box. They seemed to be communing or something, and Sara couldn't help but smile at the sight of Craig's goofy face as he baby-talked his way into the record books. She fired up a pot of coffee and brought them all a cup, happy to surrender Katie to someone else for a while.

Bad mom. That's me. Not even wanting to hold her own child.

But this was so hard. Why hadn't anyone warned her about this part?

She leaned on the doorway a minute, observed the utter chaos all around, boxes half opened, towels, dishes and clothes strewn all around the house she'd bought. Her mother had offered to help, to organize, but Sara balked, insisting she had a handle on it, unwilling to own up to how helpless she felt.

She still wasn't ready to admit defeat. That she couldn't handle her new, smelly, sleep-deprived, emotionally conflicted reality. She blinked back the tears she seemed to shed at any provocation and handed Craig and Suzanne each a mug.

Katie sat still, staring up at Craig from her vantage point on his thighs. Sara sat next to him. Suzanne sipped her coffee from her spot on a chair across the room. Sara knew something was up between them, but shoved the green-eyed monster down underneath the piles of guilt she hauled around regarding Craig.

"What are you anyway, the baby whisperer? She's been screaming at the top of her damn lungs since she got up at like six a.m. today."

"Just needed a fresh set of hands." He put an arm around her. She looked at Suzanne.

"I'm happy for you guys," she said, leaning forward to look into Suzanne's eyes.

"Thanks," the woman replied, ever the cool cucumber Sara remembered from the time she'd spent as Blake's hot and heavy, just-widowed girlfriend.

The doorbell rang again, making Katie startle and flail her arms around. Sara left Craig to comfort her, as only he seemed able to do, and answered it. Blake and Rob stood, bottle of red wine and Chinese takeout in hand. Ignoring the part of her that had hoped for a different face at the door, she smiled and let them in.

Rob opened some moving boxes and found a few juice glasses. He produced a corkscrew from his pocket and poured four glasses. Blake pulled the greasy containers from bags and rustled around in another box for utensils, unwilling to meet Rob's eyes. He'd flinched when he saw Suzanne here. He knew it. Rob knew it. But he was sick of his own weakness when it came to her. He met Rob's gaze.

"What?" he asked, knowing damn well what but unable to speak it.

Before he could blink, Rob grabbed him, held him close, pressed firm lips over Blake's. He sighed and wrapped his arms around the man who'd saved him from himself years ago.

"There. That's more like it, no?" Rob smiled, his dark eyes twinkling. Blake had never felt better. The fact that the woman who'd broken his heart sat out there in his own sister's living room, likely on the verge of a relationship with the guy who could be the father of his niece, was beyond weird. But no longer under his skin, like it had been once.

"Our soap opera continues." He elbowed Rob out of the way, opened all the containers, and found paper plates Sara must have bought as a stopgap until she could get unpacked. He watched Rob's broad shoulders and strong back and had to stop himself from reaching out for more. "I love you." He contented himself with this.

Rob turned. "Let's go play uncle a while, get it out of our collective systems."

"Already on it." Blake loved holding Katie. Between him and Craig, they formed a two-man front against the afternoons and evenings of colic that had developed in the previous weeks. He plucked Katie off Craig's lap, patted Sara's head, and smiled at Suzanne before whisking the baby back to her room.

He took a deep sniff of Katie's head. Closed his eyes as she batted at his nose, her perfect face breaking into a grin. "I love you," he whispered.

Rob smiled and took Katie from his arms, did an efficient diaper change, and laid her in the crib. "You have to let her work through some of this herself." Blake lingered, watching as his niece rooted around, settling herself for sleep. His chest constricted at the sight. He couldn't explain why. Rob put an arm around him. "Your sister I mean. Not Katie." Blake sighed and stepped away.

"Is there anything I can do right relative to my sister in your eyes?" Anger surged through him. Rob stood, his eyes calm.

"Yes. You can." He took Blake's hand and pulled him close again. "Sorry. Let's go feed everybody."

Sara watched them go, observed the give and take between her brother, his lover, and his former girlfriend. Suddenly so tired she couldn't keep her eyes open, she leaned over on Craig's shoulder. He and Suzanne and Rob chatted, none of which she heard anymore.

A set of arms lifted her. She struggled to wake up, to play hostess. "Shh," a voice whispered. "I've got you."

"Jack?" She put her arms around his neck, leaned into his chest, which rumbled with amusement.

"No, honey, it's Rob. But I can call him if you want me to." She sighed as he laid her on the bed, pulling covers up under her chin.

"No, he won't come." She opened her eyes and spotted Rob perched on the edge of the bed. Blake came up behind him and put both arms around his neck. She covered her eyes, hiding the inevitable tears. Jack had been scarce while her parents hovered, stopping in twice, only to back away, seemingly intimidated by Katie's small, needy self. Rob ran a hand down her face.

"Let me call him."

"No!" She surprised herself with her vehemence. If he didn't want any part of her life anymore, well, fine. Screw him. She rolled over. "

"Wake me up when she cries or my boobs may explode."

"TMI, sister dear." Blake tugged Rob to his feet.

Sara drifted off, her dreams a jumble of babies, pain, stress, and Jack.

Rob sighed and leaned back into Blake's embrace as they watched Sara drift off. "I should call Jack. This is killing him."

"What did you just say to me about coddling her?" Blake pressed a kiss to Rob's shoulder.

"I'm not coddling her. I'm trying to get her to talk sense. To let Jack in."

"It's a free country. Jack can drive over here and knock on the door just like the rest of us did. Jesus, we have a frigging small town cocktail party out there already."

"He feels shut out. Not needed. Although we can thank ourselves for that."

"What are you, Jack's therapist?"

Rob sighed. "Don't be a dick."

"Sorry."

"You can't do this for her." Rob disentangled himself.

Blake stuck his hands in his pockets. "I'm not. I'm helping her. I'm allowed."

"I get that. But she's keeping Jack at arm's length and he's intimidated by the baby. It makes him feel inadequate and helpless. I mean, he's busy now, trying to manage the entire company. He's used to being needed. So he's channeling it into work."

"I repeat. He's free to come over here anytime."

The doorbell rang. Rob chuckled. "And like that, he is summoned."

"Kinda like Satan."

Rob punched Blake in the arm. Sara mumbled. Blake leaned down and kissed her cheek before backing out and closing the door to her room.

By the time they wandered back into the living room, Jack had settled into one of the large chairs draped with cloth diapers doubling as spit-up towels. The tension that might have presented itself in a room containing two men who had once loved the same woman seemed blessedly absent.

"Thanks for coming, Jack." Blake took a seat opposite him. Rob shot him an odd look.

He glanced at his phone, then tucked it into his inside jacket pocket. The new lines of exhaustion lining Jack's eyes weren't lost on Blake.

"Sure. What's up?"

"I wanted us to talk about how we're going to handle things going forward."

Suzanne shifted in her seat. Craig draped an arm around her shoulders. Blake stared at Jack, but the room stayed quiet.

"She wants to go back to work in a few weeks, but I don't think Katie should go to a group daycare."

"What exactly are you proposing?" Rob's voice was tight. Blake didn't look at him.

"I was wondering if we could convince her to hire a nanny or something."

"It's Sara's baby. She's made that clear to the rest of us. What part of it are you not getting?" Jack kept his voice light.

Rob stood and walked out of the room, palpable anger trailing in his wake. Blake ignored his exit. "I promised her I'd help with this. So this is me helping, okay?"

Suzanne leaned forward and put a hand on his knee. He flinched, but she kept it there.

"Blake, I know you want to help her, but she's got to get through some of this on her own. Your need to smooth everything out isn't helping her."

He stood and started pacing the small room. "I'll tell you what, then. If you guys all think I'm wrong, then forget I said anything."

Jack rose and stood in Blake's path, hands on his shoulders. "I'll help you. I don't want the baby in some germ-infested room with half-trained teenagers in charge."

"Jack!" Suzanne leaned back. "Since when are you an expert on day care?"

He glared at her, then turned back to Blake.

"But you have to back off a little bit, man. Suzanne is right. Sara has to work her way through this on her own. It's what she wanted, remember? I'll help you convince her. She can pay for it. Think that will fly with her?" He glanced at Craig, who nodded. "I gotta go." He ran a hand through his hair.

Blake nodded. "Thanks Jack. It's a deal." Rob stood in the kitchen doorway, his gaze flat and noncommittal. Blake's heart sped up. He knew this was the right thing. Sara needed his help. He'd promised her he would. She needed him.

He dropped into a chair and watched Jack and Rob shake hands, after which Rob turned his back and returned to the kitchen without another word. The baby monitor at his elbow bleeped. He smiled as he made his way back to her room.

Screw Rob. This was his family, and he'd handle it how he wanted. He knew he'd drawn a line in the sand by not telling Rob his plan to get Jack on board with the no-daycare thing. He also knew Katie at home with a nanny meant he'd get more time with her.

The small girl flailed around, her thin cries taking hold and becoming full-fledged wails of "where the hell is my food?" Blake smiled at her. "My darling, don't cry. Uncle Blake is here for you, always." Rob appeared with a warmed bottle of Sara's breast milk, handed it to him and walked out of the room without saying a word.

Chapter Nine

Sara stared at the amazing assembly around her patio table. She took in the birthday girl—her now two-year-old daughter—sitting in her high chair giggling, the center of attention, icing smeared across her face.

Countless sleepless nights behind her, she'd jumped back into work with a vengeance. She'd even convinced Blake that Katie was ready for daycare, that she needed the social interaction with other kids to bring her down off her pedestal. Sara knew the girl was in for a surprise when she realized there were others like her, just as important in the scheme of the universe.

The weird niggling feeling that had haunted her for past few months rose again. She looked down at her hands—hands that held, soothed, changed diapers and clothes, even cooked halfway decent meals for her child. They seemed separate from her somehow.

She touched her hair. She'd gotten it cut shorter than she'd ever had it a year ago out of self-preservation. Getting up and ready for work was a virtual three-ring circus with a baby, then a toddler, in the house. Since Katie had taken to sleeping with Sara, claiming "bad dweams," it seemed easiest to just let her. But of course, all the parenting books advised against that.

All the work she'd done, all the baths taken, books read, green vegetables consumed, and she still didn't feel like a legit mother. The imposter syndrome was strong, so strong sometimes it overwhelmed her. Why she'd demanded to go down this path alone, she couldn't recall. It would have been so much easier, not to mention likely better for Katie, to just say "yes" to one of Jack's many proposals. To let him ease their way with his money and eagerness to manage everything.

The girl's squealing laughter floated in through the open window. Sara frowned. Her support group surrounding the girl had been a lifesaver, but as her work level ramped up, taking her away more evenings and weekends, she sensed the tenuous connection she'd made with her daughter slipping. Wandering back out to the patio, she observed the small girl, her light brown curls haloing around her face in the humid night, huge green eyes trained on her uncle, who would not leave her side for a second.

"Sara!" her father called from the back door. "Bourbon?"

"Cabinet in the dining room, Dad." She took a deep breath, trying to relax, but for some reason, was still on edge. "I'm worried about them." Her father stood next to her, sipping his drink.

"Yeah, he's a little obsessed, isn't he?"

Sara sighed and leaned into her father's side. "Well, I let him be, I guess. So my fault, like everything else, it seems." She turned away from the group, the sight of Craig there alone without Suzanne searing her just as deeply.

"Bake!" The little girl burbled, making the surrounding adults erupt with joy. Sara sighed, stood, and headed back inside. God knows she had enough people taking care of the child. She sighed and poured another glass of red wine.

"Hey, sexy." Jack's deep voice penetrated her self-pity party.

"When did you get here?" She ignored the zinging in her nerves at the sight of him. He'd been absent for the better part of Katie's first years. Never mind how much she needed him.

Never mind that I never asked him for help. What's he supposed to do? Read my mind?

"Just now. Seems like the birthday girl has her audience. Thought I'd find you instead." Sara closed her eyes. How did he know? He handed her a bouquet of wild flowers and a bottle of her favorite Pinot Noir.

"Nothing for Her Highness?" Sara heard the whiney tone in her voice and tried to quell it. She was certain no other mom in the universe ever resented anything about their own child. It was one more thing she sucked at.

"Of course." He pulled a present from behind his back. "Where?"

"Out there." She gestured to the open French door. He smiled and set it on the kitchen counter.

"Are you trying to get in my pants? If you are, you're scoring pretty high so far. Granted, I'm desperate." He laughed, a deep, throaty sound she associated with a different life, a different era. The "before baby Sara."

"No. Not really. Although, I wouldn't turn it down. Here, let's open this." He pulled the cork from the pinot, grabbed two glasses, and filled them. Ecstatic noises floated in from the patio.

"Thanks."

He leaned in close. Too close. She shut her eyes and stepped away. If she didn't, she'd give in, cave to the one thing she wanted, the thing she'd missed out on for years, thanks to her own stubbornness.

"You look great." He lifted his glass to her.

"Thanks."

"Sara?" Rob peeked in, saw Jack, and smiled. "Hey, Gordon."

"Hey."

Sara sipped her wine. Jack held out his hand. Sara took it and they wandered outside to many cheers and cries of "Ma! Ma!" from the little girl.

By midnight, the crowd had dispersed but for Jack, Blake and Rob. Sara sat, feet tucked up under her, as Blake put the snoozing Katie to bed. Jack sat next to her. When he'd put a hand on her leg at one point for emphasis, a quick thrill of desire shot through her.

She leaned away, catching Blake's eye. He winked. She frowned.

"Okay, I'm done." Rob stood and stretched. "Gordon, behave yourself."

Jack stood and shook his hand. Sara watched them, a sudden need to make them stay rushed through her. But she sat, accepted Blake's and Rob's kisses, and watched Jack show them to the door. He returned, a fresh glass of wine in hand.

"So," he began. Sara refused to look at him. Finally alone with him, the last two years of sleep-deprived chaos, and a distinct lack of male company were making her dizzy. "I have a proposal for you."

She kept silent but the "yes" was on her lips, if he would only ask.

He moved to one of the large leather chairs opposite her, contemplating his wine glass. "Sara, would you do me the honor of..."

She looked at him, but his gaze remained neutral, non-committal. "What? Spit it out already."

"Of taking on the management role at the downtown Stewart Realty Office."

She blinked, pretty sure she'd not heard him correctly. "Uh, what?"

"I haven't been able to replace Pam. The place has been in total shit show for over a year now."

Sara sipped and watched him, willing herself to stay seated.

"Not what I was expecting."

Jack raised an eyebrow, which sent a chill down Sara's spine. Had she truly lost him?

Whose fault is that? You pushed him away. Insisted on your independence. Get a grip.

She unfolded her legs from underneath her and propped them on the glass-topped coffee table.

He kept his gaze trained on her as he spoke. "Let's just say I got your message. Loud and clear. You should be proud."

"I'm not." She tried not to pout.

"So, about that proposal..."

Sara patted the couch next to her. "Come back over here. I think better when you're close to me."

He sank onto the couch, draping an arm around her. She snuggled into his side, forcing out all the guilt over how her need to do this mom thing on her own had affected so many lives.

"Okay, I'm here. Well?"

She closed her eyes when his lips touched her hair.

She put a hand on his thigh, relishing the familiar musculature beneath his jeans. He shifted.

"Listen, Sara, I don't know where your head is right now, but... whoa..."

In one quick move, she was on his lap, straddling him, her face inches from his. She bit her lip. Jack clutched her hips but didn't speak.

"Okay, if you insist." He cupped the back of her neck and pulled her in for a kiss that started slow, easy, intimate, before turning into something much more. The room dimmed around her.

She threaded her hands in his hair, sucked in huge breaths of him, ran her tongue across the rough rasp of his jaw, down his neck. "God, Jack, I miss you."

"Don't ruin this by talking," he growled in her ear, yanked up her t-shirt and flipped open her bra in one motion. He cupped a breast, holding it almost reverently, before lowering his lips to her nipple. The second he touched her and started lapping around the stiffened peak, she sighed.

"Oh my God, I think I just came."

He laughed into her flesh, then pushed her to her feet, shoved her skirt up and slid her panties down to her ankles. "Wait," she said. She ran into her room and snagged a god-knows-how-old condom from her bedside table drawer. He took it and rolled it down his cock.

"Resume your position?" His crooked smile almost broke her heart. But her body overruled the emotion, pushing her forward, back onto his lap. The sensation of his erection against her bare flesh brought fresh moans to her lips.

"Do it again," she whispered.

"Are you sure you want to go here, Sara?" His eyes were like a midnight sky, just as she remembered. "Because I'm not inclined to fuck and run." He groaned as she reached down to unzip him, fisting his hard flesh. "Although a fuck would be nice."

He flipped them around so fast Sara squealed, putting a hand over her mouth as he dove back down to her nipples, caressing, sucking, licking, making her back arch, her entire body throb with need. She sensed the pulse of their years' long connection swirling around them, making her head spin as he kissed her and kissed her.

"I need this. So much," she muttered into his lips. He started to pull away, but she gripped his face. "I need you, Jack. Please. I..."

"Say it," he said, jaw clenching. She shifted her hips, tilted them so she could feel his flesh against hers. Tears stung the back of her eyes as he lifted up and away from her, his hand on the amazing part of him that she wanted inside her. She reached up and yanked him back down, her lips near his ear.

"I'm sorry. I miss you. I need you."

He groaned and pressed into her with one firm thrust. She wrapped her legs around him, needing every inch of him inside her.

"Sara," he whispered, his exhalations against her lips. "Look at me." She stared at him, the hard reality of their inevitable physical connection ramping up, making them both breathless. But instead of saying anything, including the three words she wanted to hear him say, he closed his eyes, thrust hard, shuddered, and came just as the world exploded behind her eyes.

Her body clenched and pulsed with orgasmic energy. They continued moving together for a few more seconds. When guilt rushed in to fill the void in her chest, she shoved it back, sighed and kissed him, slow and easy. He slipped from her body and sat, gasping. "Damn. I've lost my touch. What was that, all of five seconds?" He got up to dispose of the rubber.

"No, you haven't." She stretched and put her legs on his lap after he sat back down.

"Ma?"

Jack jumped up, yanking his jeans up and tossing a blanket over Sara as she scrambled to reassemble her clothes. She rose, keeping the blanket wrapped around her. The little girl stood, ratty stuffed animal clutched in one hand, tears in her eyes.

"Bad dweam," she blurted, before she started wailing. Sara scooped her up, making soothing noises, got her a glass of water and tucked her back in, ignoring the girl's cries for "Bwake," reminding her that Uncle Blake had gone home to his house.

She sighed and tugged on a pair of old jeans and a t-shirt, regret weighing heavy on her. They shouldn't have done that. She and Jack had no business rekindling anything, much less their undeniable physical attraction.

"Hey." He stood in the door, redressed, looking perfect. "Everything okay?" He eyed the sleeping girl as if staring at a circus sideshow. Anger zinged through her. It was almost a relief—and gave her an excuse.

"Yeah. Let's go back out." He followed her. A strange new awkwardness between them made her gut roll. She ran a hand through her hair.

"I'm sorry. I don't know what came over me, I mean, earlier." She looked up at the ceiling, then leveled her gaze at him. Jack Gordon. The man of her dreams, sometimes nightmares. The guy she'd learned to love, to trust, to want.

But she'd been so strong for the past couple of years, keeping him at arm's length. Growing stronger as a single mom with every passing day. There was no need for a man in her life.

"I'm sorry. I shouldn't have... we shouldn't have."

"I agree."

She shut her eyes, forgetting how much she counted on him to talk her out of it. His agreeing with her wasn't what she wanted. She gripped the edge of the sink.

Stop it Sara. Grow up. You're a parent now. Stop acting like a horny teenager.

"Then go." She didn't turn around as she spoke. "We got our itches scratched. No more, no less. Thanks." She turned to face him. Holding back the compulsion that screamed in her ear to grab him, hold on to him, let him be what he wanted to be for her, she swallowed hard and tried to smile. Because this was right. They couldn't be together. It was be a giant disaster.

He blinked, then left without a word. Sara's water glass made a satisfying crash in the sink.

"Ma!" the voice called again and Sara trudged back to her room, "sorry" on her lips.

Chapter Ten

Blake looked up from the spreadsheets on his laptop when Rob tossed his keys on the counter. Smiling, he accepted a kiss and then bent back to the work at hand.

"I have a surprise for you." Rob stated, after pouring a glass of orange juice.

"Hmm?" Blake didn't pay attention. He frowned when Rob snapped his laptop shut on his fingers. "Hey. I'm working here."

"I said, I have a surprise for you." Blake leaned back, admiring the tall, handsome blonde man with whom he shared his life and business. Rob flipped Blake's computer back open, punched a few keys, and turned it back around to face him. A huge, luxurious looking boat sailing along an astonishing blue sea flashed up on the screen.

"Nice."

"Yes, it will be. Your passport is up to date, right?"

Blake frowned at him.

"I can't go anywhere right now."

"Why not?" Rob rubbed his shoulders, easing out tension with every stroke.

"Well, for starters, I just hired a new brewer, and I don't think he has a good handle on things. Oh yes, right there." He leaned back into Rob's body to let the man work the stress out of him. "And Katie needs..." Blake's chair almost toppled backwards at the sudden absence of anyone behind it. "What?"

Rob glared at him, shut the computer and walked out.

Sara glanced at her phone, saw it was Rob and answered as she attempted to navigate her way through the latest crisis du jour in the office she now managed. Because she had said yes to that proposal of Jack's. He was now the general sales manager of the entire company, and she managed the brokerage's most successful branch. So she guessed he was her boss.

Which put him at a convenient distance.

Email had been flying fast and furious over a deal gone sour. She was trying to handle it without pulling Jack into the mix. She set the phone down and hit speaker so she could multitask. At the clipped sound of his first words, she stopped and picked it back up.

"What's wrong Rob? Is Blake…"

"You and I need to talk."

"Okay." She reached over to shut her door, curious but not too worried. Rob had been such an anchor for her brother for so long. Whatever it was, she remained confident he could handle it.

"I need Blake to take a vacation with me, Sara, but he won't because he thinks he has to be responsible for Katie."

She frowned. She'd never heard the tone he was using. Anger suffused every word, making its way into her brain and igniting a small fire of defensiveness.

"I don't know what you…"

"Yes. You do. You have got to stop relying on him so much, Sara. It's not good for your relationship with your daughter. And it's playing fucking hell with my relationship with your brother."

"But…"

"Listen, I love you. I love Katie. But God dammit, I love Blake more, okay? He's set himself up to be way too responsible for Katie. He started out that way. I let him do it. But now it's got to stop."

"I'm sorry Rob." A rush of guilt filled her brain. She relied on him too much, but Blake made himself available, insisting she work whatever hours she needed to, that he had Katie under control. And he did. "You're right," she admitted.

"I know I'm right. Now call him and tell him if he doesn't come on this vacation with me, I may move out. I'm not kidding." She stared at the phone that had gone dead in her hand. Shaking, holding back tears, she hit Blake's speed dial.

"Yeah?" He sounded pissed.

"Honey, you have to listen to me now…"

Chapter Eleven

Jack stared at the computer screen, trying to absorb the chart his new secretary had prepared. He gave up after a few minutes, exhausted by the myriad bullshit details he now had to sweat. Named general manager of the Stewart Realty Empire over two years ago, he still couldn't wrap his mind around all the added stress. At the time, it had seemed like the perfect solution to take his mind off the daily dilemma. The woman he loved beyond reason, refusing to acknowledge him, and the distinct and alarming lack of sexual activity that followed.

He'd been mistaken.

In hindsight, it probably hadn't been the best idea to convince her to take on the sales manager's job at the downtown office, which forced them together on a near daily basis, almost always under stressful circumstances. Head pounding, he slammed the laptop shut.

"Jack?" Jason poked his head in the new office, "We need to focus on…"

Jack held up a hand. He was through for the day. Period. He'd spent a horrific morning dodging bullets from lame-ass attorneys trying to press bogus lawsuits on a couple of his agents for misrepresentation and had presided over a rancorous management meeting in which he'd been assaulted on all sides. The icing on the cake was Sara in her full-throated fury at him for cutting her office's budget for things like the premium coffee and cable on all those frigging electricity-sucking televisions.

"You might as well shut us down and stick me out in a shitty strip mall, Jack. I gotta have this stuff. People expect it. We look cheap otherwise and my clients want their downtown office equipped with locally sourced coffee and ESPN. You get me?"

He'd reminded her—through gritted teeth—that because he understood exactly how much that fucking showpiece of an office cost to run every month, there would be changes. She'd have to get creative. It was that, or he'd have to increase each of her agents' desk fees, the monthly amount each agent paid the company to cover stuff like printing and, in her case, premium cable and fancy coffee.

His teeth ached, watching the costs rising every month. Making the situation worse, it was happening in conjunction with a leveling-off of high-end sales from that branch. He made it clear he wouldn't continue to fund the toys and premium caffeine unless her sales numbers came up.

The meeting had gone downhill from there.

She'd been a perfect manager so far—tough, but approachable, firm, but fair. She'd get her head around it soon and start cranking out revenue, but having to work with her every day ripped his guts out.

He'd offered to take her out on dates, only half-kidding about quick jaunts to Paris or Rome. She'd laugh, remind him she couldn't afford a babysitter, and go back to ignoring him. Or biting his fucking head off. Which reminded him all over again that she was right. They had less than zero business being together.

He ran a hand down his face, tried to forget the moment they'd shared at her house a couple of years ago. Since then, he'd found a willing woman or two to take his edge off. He'd caved that night on her couch out of pure physical need, but it had left himself wide open for her rejection. Something he had no interest in experiencing ever again.

The dates had proved to be just that–nothing but physical release. He was sick of them, and himself, already.

Yet, even with all of that, the sight of her name on an incoming text still made him smile.

"Hey, Blake and Rob are on vacation. Can you pick up Katie from daycare?"

He frowned. The baby years had flown by in a blur of diapers, breast milk and avoidance on his part. Babies made him nervous, period. He recognized his own lameness, but it seemed she had plenty of help from family and Craig. Although since being accepted to medical school down in Nashville, he'd been of less use.

Jack had always felt like a fifth wheel around the kid, with so many people involved in her day-to-day care. Ashamed to acknowledge he didn't even know where "daycare" was, he agreed, got the details and headed out.

He parked at the daycare building—which was a total zoo by the time he arrived—and followed Sara's instructions about going to the main office to present his identification, since he'd never picked Katie up before. Little kids swarmed through the huge hallway, screeching, and flinging themselves into their parents' arms. The place reeked of pee and stale lunch boxes.

By the time he completed the annoying paperwork, it had more or less cleared out. He stood, like a chastened schoolboy, in front of the director's desk as she called Sara to confirm that he, one Mr. Jack Gordon, said with a long appraising look at him and his drivers' license, had been authorized to retrieve one Miss Katherine Elizabeth Thornton.

He adjusted his tie, nervous about having her in his car, worried he hadn't installed the car seat he'd retrieved from Sara's office the right way. Not to mention a whole host of shit he couldn't even begin to name. The main worry about coming face-to-face with Katie.

He hadn't seen her in months. Would she even recognize him?

He glanced around, still waiting for them to copy his ID and, if the time commitment was any sign, to do a federal background check on him. Anger replaced anxiety as his patience waned. He tapped his foot.

"Look, I'm good, okay. I'm her…" He stopped dead. The woman at the desk looked up. "Uncle." His voice faded.

"Katie certainly has a lot of those," the annoying person chirped before handing his ID back and pointing to a side door. She gave him a different sort of look. This one he recognized. He smiled at her. "You gay like her other uncles?"

"Nope."

"Well then." Her eyes flicked up and down his suit-clad form. He made a point to take his hands out of his pockets to display his ring-less state, ignoring the anxiety that had reasserted itself, falling into flirt mode as self-defense mechanism.

"So, this is your place?" He gestured around.

"Yes, I own it." She leaned back and crossed her long legs. He took a step closer.

"You have kids then?"

"Older ones." Her eyes swept up and down him. He chuckled.

"You realize you're checking me out, right?"

"Yeah, I do." She slid a business card across her desk at him. "Go ahead through there. She's waiting."

The place practically echoed, all the commotion having died down. Now there was only an eerie silence. He didn't see a soul. About to start back through the door to the office and rip somebody a new one for sending him on a wild goose chase, he stopped in his tracks at the sound of a small voice.

"Who are you?"

He stepped closer, letting the light hit his face. "I'm your Uncle Jack. Where are you, anyway?"

"Where's Uncle Blake?" He peered around a bookshelf and saw her sitting on a small table, matching lunchbox and backpack clutched to her chest. Her bright white, high-top tennis-shoe-clad feet swung back and forth. Jack took in the hot pink tutu, purple tights and orange t-shirt adorned with what looked like a sponge, with a face.

"He's on vacation. Nice outfit."

He held back, hands in pockets. Her huge green eyes appraised him with a worldliness that startled him. Tufts of dark blonde hair had escaped their braids and haloed her face. The resemblance to her mother, all the way down to the attitude she wore like a glove, was eerie in the extreme.

"Thanks. It's my favorite. Are you Stranger Danger? You have on a nice suit for a kid-lapper." She didn't move from her perch, just kept staring at him, her gaze open and innocent. A weird feeling settled in Jack's chest as he watched her feet swinging back and forth. He took a seat next to her.

"Thanks. It's my favorite. I'm not a stranger. Or a kidnapper. I've been to your house before, for, um, birthdays and stuff like that. I'm taking you home today."

"Oh, okay. Hang on." He watched, incredulous, as she pulled a sparkling pink phone from her bag and put it to her ear. He cocked an eyebrow at her, listening as she called Sara, getting confirmation that Uncle Jack did not represent stranger danger.

"Your mother gave you a phone? Pretty advanced for a four-year-old, wouldn't you say?" He smiled when she jumped down and stuck her hand out. He took it.

"Yes, but I can only call, not text or use internets or anything. No games either. And I am five years old." She pouted a half second. "Mommy says it makes me in-pe-den-dant. Pleased to meet you, Uncle Jack. Can we get Washtenaw Dairy on the way home? Please?" He kept her small, warm hand in his and led her out.

"Won't that ruin your dinner?"

"If Mommy's running late, then you have to feed me dinner, anyway. Uncle Blake makes me homemade mac and cheese. Can you make that?" Jack shook his head. The girl's face brightened. "I know! Let's have ice cream for dinner."

"Quite the negotiator. You're more like your mommy than you realize." He fastened her into the complex seat with her help.

"I get that a lot."

Jack laughed, loving the sound when she joined him. "How old are you, anyway? Twenty? Thirty?"

"No silly. I'm five and one quarters. How old are you? A hundred?"

"Ha! Only at night."

"Huh?"

"Never mind. I haven't had ice cream for dinner in a while. Let's make that happen." He put the car in gear and headed toward the venerable Ann Arbor ice cream spot nestled in the residential Old West Side. He snuck glances at her in the rearview mirror as she kept up a stream-of-consciousness monologue about the relative merits of Sponge Bob Square Pants versus Steven Universe, whatever those were. He smiled. His life would never be the same again, and he'd never been happier.

Chapter Twelve

Sara re-opened the car door, yanked her coattail out, and noted Jack's car parked in front of her house. She took a breath. The stressful day crashed in on her, making her long for an enormous glass of wine and a bit of quiet. But coaxing Katie into the tub, endless rounds of book reading and excuses for not going to bed, then yet more hours of work still lay ahead of her.

She leaned on the car, chastising herself, and wishing Blake were here. She shoved that away, remembering her promise to herself about not relying on him so much.

"Be the mom," Rob had said when she dropped them off at the airport. "You can do it. You have to do it."

It was depressing how many people who loved her, though she couldn't handle "being the mom." She sometimes wondered if she'd be that worst of clichés—the self-fulfilling prophecy when it came to parenthood success or lack thereof. Katie was a great kid—smarter for her own good, but she came by that honestly enough. They'd survived the toddler years, and she seemed fairly well ensconced in her life as Boss of the Montessori Pre-School Class. Sara was inundated with requests for playdates, not to mention wine dates with the moms.

Maybe she'd done something right with the girl. She loved her, so much so it was a physical pain. Like when they'd sing their way to day care or went on a rare mother/daughter weekend picnic. The pretty, precocious, clever, somewhat manipulative little girl was her heart, ripped out of her chest, walking around outside her body unprotected.

Motherhood. It's a brutal business.

She headed through the side door, noting as she did every day that the damn thing needed a coat of paint. The kitchen was dark and spotless, obviously untouched for dinner. She frowned, putting her briefcase and purse on the counter.

Music wafted through the house. The sound of Jack's laughter from upstairs made her squeeze her eyes shut for a second. She'd missed him so much. Although, she would never in a million years admit that to anyone, much less to him. Not marrying him was the smartest and hardest thing she'd ever done in her life.

Her daughter's loud giggle echoed down the steps. Sara smiled, poured herself a cabernet and sipped while slipping out of her shoes on the way to the living room, thanking god that it was cleaning service day.

She sank into the cream-colored leather couch, trying to relax, listening to the sounds of Katie babbling away, mixed with Jack's rumbling, regular replies. After about thirty minutes, the noises ceased. She closed her eyes, relishing the concept of not being in charge at least for a few more minutes even though the ever present guilt was hard on the heels of that.

A hand on her knee woke her. Her eyes flew open, panic filling her brain. She put her glass on the table and got up, starting to the steps on autopilot.

"She's asleep, although the ice cream and donut dinner might lead to a tummy ache later. Sorry in advance."

A fire danced in the grate. He'd poured himself a glass of wine and sat, dress shirt loosened at the neck, sleeves rolled up on a shirt that looked like he'd given a dog a bath, not an almost five-year-old girl. She slumped against the wall, using every ounce of willpower she had not to launch herself into his arms. He raised his glass.

"Well done, Sara. She's an amazing kid."

"She has been from the start. It's me as a mom that I worry about. I mean, you've probably figured out that she's kind of..."

"Mature for her age? Yeah. I get that." He rose to his full height, bringing her heart into her throat. "You're gonna have a hell of a time keeping me away now." He walked by her, not touching or speaking. She sighed, knowing she didn't deserve any different.

She followed him into the kitchen and watched him refill his glass. He turned, pinning her with his familiar, deep blue gaze.

"I want to take her with me to Orlando next week. I'm meeting Mo and the kids there. Brandis has a short leave to the states, so we planned..."

"Are you nuts?" She only half meant it. But she sensed the control she had over the situation slipping from her.

Why not trade one uncle for another, a tiny voice whispered.

No. This is my daughter. Our life. I won't let him swoop in and take over.

She glared at him. "You can't do that. She has a schedule. A routine."

"She's four years old, for Christ's sake. I'll be sure and put it on her secretary's calendar." He kept his face neutral, but she sensed anger on the horizon. She dug her heels in, not really sure why, but needing to assert herself. This was it. This was the moment. The moment Jack took over.

"No."

"Why not? Jealous? I can take you, too."

She stepped away from him. "She doesn't know you. I mean, what kind of mother would let her daughter go off to Florida with some... guy she hardly knows?"

He frowned and her scalp prickled in that familiar way, anticipating a fight.

"I'm not some guy." He gripped her arm as she tried to walk past him. "And you fucking well know it."

"I'll think about it." She yanked out of his grip and walked to her bedroom, stripped out the suit she felt like she'd been wearing for a week, and tugged on sweatpants and a ratty t-shirt. As she yanked her hair up in a ponytail, she berated herself.

Stop it Sara. Don't be such a hypocrite. You pushed him away on purpose. Give him a break. Stop acting surprised that he's smitten with the girl.

The older Katie got, the more of Jack's personality she saw in her. The kid was organized to the point of painful, tidy, neat, and eager to be in control of everything around her.

But she's your child. You get to say no to an Orlando trip.

To her surprise, Jack had his coat back on and keys in hand by the time she made her way back downstairs. She tried not to let her disappointment show.

"So, thanks. For today." Face neutral, she brushed past him on her way to the kitchen.

"No problem." He stayed put. She leaned against the kitchen counter. "You think I'm kidding."

She raised an eyebrow. "About what?"

"About dislodging me from your life now that I've met... your daughter and spent some time with her." He stared at her. Then, before she could blink, he had her in his arms. His lips hovered over hers. She tried to calm her pounding heart, realizing her deep well of desire for the man holding her right now.

"Jack." She made a half-hearted attempt to pull away. "Don't..."

... ever let me go...

He put a finger over her lips. "I won't." He brought his face close. "But I won't be denied my daughter. Are we clear?" Sara gasped when he stepped away. "I'll let you continue to delude her into thinking I'm yet another uncle. But I'm doing that for her sake, not yours."

She tried to speak, but no words formed. Until something horrible flooded her brain, a fear of losing Katie forever that left her cold and shaking. He chuckled, but his eyes stayed dark with anger.

"Don't worry, dear. I won't press the issue. I don't need a paternity test to know that's my child asleep in the other room. But you'll have to adjust your damnable independence a little." He ran a finger down her face. "You and I need to learn how to get along, at least in front of her. Because I will be allowed into her life."

"You have no say in this." Her whole body ached to have him close, but her mind wouldn't let her yield. Too many years of denial and anger between them, perhaps, but there it was.

"Actually I do. I won't make you prove anything. We'll just have a quiet understanding between us. Got it?" He kissed her then, without preamble, and with an urgency that made her moan as he pressed her against the kitchen counter. He tore his lips from hers and stepped back. "I'll pick her up again tomorrow. We'll talk more then." And with that, he was gone, the door making an annoying soft click behind him.

She shook with fury, remorse, and a weird sense of relief. She'd been holding herself together for almost five years, operating under a strange sort of immaculate conception myth in her own head. As she watched his car pull out of her driveway, the small kernel of hope that maybe, now, they could make something different work nestled deep in her soul.

Why he'd even want her was anyone's guess, of course. She'd been so adamant, so stubborn. If he demanded significant time with the girl, she'd allow it. Encourage it, even.

But would it be too late?

She stood for almost fifteen minutes, staring in the mirror at her face that she'd washed, toned, moisturized. She touched her cheek. Ran a fingertip across her lips and down her neck.

Jack. He loved her and she needed to cut the crap and admit it.

Her heart raced. A metal band wrapped around her chest, tightening with her every inhale. Her face flushed. She put her hand to her neck. Tears spilled from her eyes, dropping onto the marble vanity top.

Oh God. Could she do this? Could she trust him? Or would it be the dumbest decision she ever made for her and her daughter?

"Shit. Fuck. Goddamn it all to hell and back... Gah!" Jack pounded the steering wheel all the way home from Sara's house. An incoming call dinged through the radio. He glanced down and saw Evan's name on the screen. He hit the answer button on the steering wheel.

"What?"

"In civilized countries, we say 'hello' when answering the phone."

His friend's voice was light, but Jack sensed something was wrong.

"Fuck off. I'm in a shitty mood."

"Good. Me too. It's why I'm calling."

His house was cold and empty, and it pissed him off to no end. His psyche couldn't take much more. Total abstinence from sex of all kinds, vanilla and otherwise, made him want to leap out of his skin. The few women he'd taken on perfunctory dates just to get off later danced through his head. His balls ached and his head pounded. He jerked the shower on full force and stepped into the burning hot streams coming at him from above and both sides.

By the time he got out, fury made the room dim. He flopped down on the bed, ran his hand up and down his stubborn erection, and proceeded to relieve a bit of stress so he could at least walk. Wandering downstairs, he noted the time and wished he could talk to his sister. Then again, she'd brow beat him for being such a pussy. He sighed, grabbed his keys, and headed out to meet his friend.

"You're being a real pussy about this." Evan held up a beer bottle.

"You realize that I don't care what you think." Jack poured another splash of bourbon into his glass. The music surged and pulsed around him. Evan sighed and did the same. "What's your problem? I told you my sad sack story. It's your turn."

"Julie wants a baby. I don't. I thought she didn't. We fought. Now I'm here with you like a loser instead of home with my wife, where I fucking belong." He sighed and drained his beer, signaling for another.

"Huh." Jack sipped and stared at the stage show. It had zero effect on him. He was numb, packed in cotton, with a need so urgent to go back to Sara's right now he had to grip his thighs to keep from leaping up and running out the door. Hanging out at the area's fanciest gentlemen's club—okay, titty bar—usually lifted his mood. But right now he felt like the saddest sack on sad sack nation.

"Yeah." Evan turned to the show then too, and the men stayed silent until agreeing without speaking to leave the strip club where they'd agreed to meet.

All the way home, Jack felt dirty, slimy, coated in shame for even going there, even though the place had been his go-to for a lot of years. The thought of those women having to act the way they did just to make ends meet, feed their kids, go to school made him swear off going to any of them ever again.

Sara frowned at the unfamiliar number on her screen. She ran her fingers through her shower wet hair and answered it.

"Sara, hey. It's Julie."

"Oh, hi there." She'd met Evan and Julie a couple of times. It was all part of the complex friendship web Jack wove. The woman stayed silent. "Um. Can I help you with something?"

"I was wondering if Evan was with you. I mean, with Jack."

"Jack's not here. I can call him…"

"No. That's okay."

Sara sat, poured a glass of wine. Julie's few words spoke volumes. "Do you want to come over? I mean, we don't know each other that well, but…"

But now that I plan to do everything in my power to get Jack back, I might as well make friends with his friends. She finished in her head.

"Oh, no, that's all right."

"No, I mean it. I have some decent wine and a few snacks. Let's chat. We can compare notes on how shitty men are."

Julie laughed. "Fine. What's your address?"

Sara had never had a close female friend. She mistrusted other women, had been burned by several supposed close friends in college, and had limited her engagement with females outside of work. By the time Julie was weaving back into her kitchen to open another bottle, Sara had to concentrate to not see double. But it was fun, god damn it. And they were drunk enough to declare themselves best friends forever.

"I want a baby so bad." Julie dropped onto the couch. "You're lucky." Sara tried not to snort.

"No. Just fertile with bad timing."

"Evan was such a total shit about it tonight. Claimed I misled him. I've changed my mind, damn it. He won't listen."

Sara patted her friend's knee. "Men are total garbage. That much is true."

"Jack's cool though. I like him."

"Yeah." They sipped their wine. Sara sighed, ready to admit how she felt. "But he's wrong for me, or something. We can't seem to get it together."

"You have the perfect excuse. Why don't you just go with that? Let him be Katie's dad like he wants to be. You guys try too damn hard to find reasons not to be together. You realize that, right?"

"He's so volatile. I don't want to put her through it." Sara ignored the fact that she'd done exactly what Julie accused her of–come up with yet another excuse not to be with Jack.

Julie set her glass down on the table and leaned back, hand over her eyes. "He loves you more than anything. You'd be better off if you acknowledged it. Shit." She grabbed for her buzzing phone, leaving Sara to contemplate her words. "What? No. I'm not home. I'm out. Why? Screw you Adams I'll be out as long as I please." She ended the call. "That went well." Then she burst into tears.

Sara's phone rang. She rolled her eyes. "What are we in middle school?" she asked before Jack could say anything.

"So Julie is with you?" His voice sounded muffled.

"Yeah. She is. I'm putting her to bed on the couch."

"Okay. Thanks." He was quiet, but remained on the line.

She swallowed hard. "You can take Katie to Florida next week."

"Thank you. I appreciate it you trusting me with her."

"Like you said, we'd better figure out how to deal with each other as adults if we are gonna do this... co-parenting thing or whatever. But you stay Uncle Jack. Got it?" She closed her eyes to keep the room from spinning. It made it worse.

"Whatever you want."

"What I want is irrelevant. But this is how it has to be for now."

"I know what I want." His voice dipped low, buzzing in her ears.

Sara didn't say anything, afraid she'd blurt out something drunken and stupid.

"I want you," he declared, then he hung up.

Chapter Thirteen

The morning had started late. Sara slapped a sandwich together, added a banana and Katie's favorite chocolate chip cookies, and threw it all into her daughter's lunchbox. The girl sat perched on the kitchen counter, her usual spot, observing Sara with a critical eye. "Mommy, I don't like that kind of cookie. Here, give it to me." Sara handed the girl the lunchbox, watching as she reassembled it and added the juice box Sara had forgotten in her haste. The girl's calm, yet persistent organizational skills getting under Sara's skin in a way that shamed her at that moment.

She tried not to snap. "Come on sweetie, we're running late."

"I like Uncle Jack."

"Yes, honey. So do lots of people." She winced at her cattiness. "I mean, he's very likeable."

"He wants to take me to Disney World." Sara looked over her shoulder at the girl. Her eyes were wary, as if testing out the concept.

"Do you want to go with him?"

"I think so. I mean, if it's okay with you. That's what he said."

"It's okay with me."

"Have you gone on vacation with him before?"

Sara shivered. "Why?"

"He said you had, that you had a good time. Did you meet Mickey Mouse and have a Princess dinner? He said we would."

Sara ran a hand down her daughter's face. "No sweetie, I didn't. But you'll have a good time, I'm sure. Where's your backpack? I told you to leave it by the back door. Shit." She yelped as her toe connected with a chair leg.

"It's okay. I'm ready." And she was. Sara sighed and looked at the girl.

"I'm sorry, baby. I'm not a very good mommy sometimes."

The girl pulled her down to eye level and put her hands on Sara's shoulders. Her green-eyed gaze was serious. "You're the best mommy. Now let's go. We're late."

The afternoon had been slow, so Sara met Katie at the daycare door, hoping to surprise her. She'd spent all day pondering the girl's response to her self-centered whining about not being a good mom and had concocted some "girls' time" for them in her head, full of laughter, swings at the park, and a picnic. The disappointment on the girl's face at the sight of her put a dent in her decent mood.

"Where's Uncle Jack?" the girl demanded, crossing her arms.

"I'm here, honey. Uncle Jack just helped me out yesterday."

"I want him." She dug in her heels, her lower lips staring to quiver.

"C'mon. Let's go to the park. The one near the DQ." She held out her hand.

"No." A tear dripped off the girl's small nose. "Why do I have so many uncles, anyway?" Sara tried not to overreact.

"Because you're the luckiest girl on the planet, that's why." She scooped her up and held on tight, fighting the urge to agree with her.

Katie sniffled a little. Then smiled, putting her hands on Sara's face. "Okay. But I'll bet Uncle Jack would like to go with us to the park. Let's call him."

"Hi Mommy!" The sound of Katie's voice made Sara's eyes burn.

"Hi baby! Are you having fun?" She leaned back in the chair and let herself acknowledge that the week she thought she'd enjoy—one free of daycare drop-off or pickup, meals that balanced and the laundry required to appease Katie's fashion sense—had had the opposite effect. She'd been miserable in the empty house, wandering from room to room, tidying up, anticipating the sound of Katie's voice.

"I love it so much here! It's sunny and warm and I saw Mickey and had the Princess dinner and have been swimming and water sliding with…"

Sara let the girl's words swirl around in her brain until she interrupted the monologue. "Are you wearing sunscreen and..."

The exasperation in the girl's sigh made Sara smile. "Uncle Jack wants to talk to you." There was a rustling. Then Jack's deep voice filled her ears.

"Hey. I think it's a success. I'm officially a Walt Disney company investor by this point, if money spent at an individual resort is any sign of..."

"I miss her, Jack. So much."

He laughed. "Of course you do, dear. She's your daughter. You've been with her for her entire life. Cut yourself some slack."

A loud screech made Sara flinch. "I'll assume that's a sound of joy and not terror or pain."

"You can leave me in charge, never fear. Katie, get down off the ceiling fan."

"Jack!"

"I'm kidding. Thanks for letting her come with me. It means a lot to me. I know it was hard for you to agree to it."

"No, it wasn't. I just wanted you to work for it a little."

"That's my girl. Stubborn to the last. Gotta dash. We have a date with a mermaid or some shit."

Sara smiled. "Have fun. See you soon."

Chapter Fourteen

By the time Katie returned, Sara felt like she had a better handle on managing her office. Jack had proven true to his word—forcing her to take a hard look at her expenditures, threatening cuts and all sorts of crap. The strict, personal hands-off policy he'd adopted made her insane. Thank goodness the office sales numbers were picking up because of her focus on the bottom line. The focus he'd insisted on.

Of course, it took two to tango. It's within my power to change all this. I want to. Step the hell up. Close the gap.

But she wouldn't. The hurt of the past years ran deep and her fear of experiencing it again kept her aloof, matching his demeanor. She marched through her days, piling up victories at work, enjoying Katie in ways she hadn't in a while, but all the while wishing for one thing—for an opening from Jack.

But it appeared she'd lost her shot.

She stared at the spreadsheets in front of her, attempting to justify expenditures that exceeded all other sales offices by a lot. Lordy, management sucked. Her phone buzzed with a text from Jack.

You there? We need to talk.

She frowned at the clock. Nearly six-thirty. Julie had agreed to get Katie from daycare and the girl had been giddy at the concept of a mani/pedi with her mommy's new friend.

Yeah. For a little longer. What's up?

I'll be there in ten.

She tried not to apply lipstick or fuss with her hair. God knows he'd seen her at her absolute worst. She wasn't about to primp for him. Burying herself in the cost analysis again distracted her from the urge to pace, brush her hair, anything to look good for the man. By the time he rapped on her doorframe, she jumped in surprise.

He handed her a double skim latte—her favorite—in a cardboard cup and sank into the chair by her desk before speaking. "Fuck me running. This management thing sucks on so many levels I can't name them all." He ran a hand down his face. She grinned as she sipped the well timed caffeine.

"Yeah, and I can thank you for my role in it."

"I want to do more with Kate." She shook her head at the abrupt change of subject.

She narrowed her eyes at him, her natural reaction to resist his continued insertion in their lives. "What do you mean, more?"

"Give me some days to pick her up. Do the afternoon stuff. But on a regular basis."

"Well..."

"C'mon Sara, I'm crazy about that kid. I thought we had an understanding."

She sighed.

"I'm sort of surprised, that's all. You didn't want to have anything to do with her for so long. I don't want to confuse her with another uncle. She's already..." She stopped, not willing to let on what sort of affect he'd already had on Katie.

"I'll accept my part in that. I avoided her because you seemed to want me to. You insisted on it, if you recall. But I told you I wanted to play a bigger role. Now I'm here to sort out the details."

Sara put her feet up on her desk. But she was shaking inside, so hard she had to curl her fingers into fists and focus on not falling out of the chair. She stared at him, taking in everything about him that had compelled her to do such idiotic things. His deep blue eyes were shining with intensity, his stubbled jaw set.

This was her fault. She'd created this mess. But when she'd seen that damn plus sign on the pregnancy test pee stick, she'd closed ranks and decided to do it on her own, if for no other reason than to prove that she could. And in the process, she'd alienated the handsome, care-taking man across from her right now.

"This is out of the blue, isn't it?"

"No. It's not, and you know it." He mirrored her, propping his own feet up on the opposite of hers. They sat in silence.

"Jack, you're…"

"Persistent? Incredibly talented? Still madly in love with you despite the obvious signs I'm a fool?"

She laughed, relieved, but unable to respond the way she should. "Stubborn?"

"Hello, kettle, this is pot. Guess what color you are?" He grinned over his cup at her, setting her nerve endings jangling. "I miss you Sara." Those simple words, said countless times before, had a different effect on her today.

She stood and walked around to face him, leaning on the desk. He looked up at her. The space between them crackled with energy. She took one step past him and shut her door, then stood, hands on hips.

"Okay, persistent. And definitely talented… at a lot of things." Putting her hands on the arms of the chair, she leaned in and touched her lips to his. He stayed still, letting her lead. So she did.

She licked his lips, parted them with her tongue, their only contact by mouth but with more than enough between them to fill a book. She sighed when he yanked her down to his lap, forcing her to straddle him, digging his fingers into her hips.

He buried his hands in her hair, pulled hard, making her gasp. When his lips and teeth touched her neck, she had to hold back a yelp of pleasure. She gasped as his hands roamed up and down her back, tugging her skirt up and cupping her ass. But she had no words. She grasped for them, but found nothing to express her convoluted feelings. She went with how damn good it felt to have his hands on her again and worry about everything else later.

"What do you want from me, really?" His words were muffled, his mouth staying pressed to her neck, then down between her breasts. "Because I can give you this." He clutched her ass, grinding his obvious arousal against her. "And this." He yanked her blouse up, freed one breast, ran his thumb across her nipple.

He stopped and cradled her face between his hands, making her look into his eyes. "But that it's not enough for me now. I want more." He pushed her up and off him, confusing her as her body continued to thrum and pulse with the kind of anticipation only Jack could provide. He stood and stuck his hands in his pockets.

Sara caught her breath, and in a split second had herself wrapped around the tall, firm body she still dreamed of, covered the firm lips she fantasized about to that very day. He groaned, met her halfway, and the world drowned in her sea of lust, frustration and something deeper. She forced that aside. Their teeth clicked, tongues tangled with urgency.

But he broke away and took two huge steps back from her. She could see his jaw clenching. Recalled the rasp of his late-day stubble against her skin. She took a deep breath, marveling at the intensity of their connection for the millionth time.

"Dear God, Sara, I need to be inside you, to taste you, to fuck you. I need it so badly I can't breathe. But we have to stop."

"No," she whispered. "You don't want to. I don't want to." But she kept her distance. He was right. This, right here, right now, had to stop. Communication by random hook ups was no way to live. Despite how much her entire soul clamored for said hook up with the man standing at the opposite end of her office from her, looking at her like a starving man might eyeball a steak dinner.

"No, baby, I don't want to." Jack ran a shaking hand down his face and across his lips, furious with himself and with her.

Which was a pretty apt description of their basic issue. Neither of them would admit how good it felt to be together. How much they both wanted it. Something encoded in their respective DNA wouldn't allow it and kept them both clinging to old arguments, old scripts, old bullshit.

He did a mental shuffle for an excuse and grabbed onto something so lame even he couldn't believe he said it. "If you must know, I don't carry rubbers around with me anymore. And last I checked, the lack of a condom is how we landed in this particular quandary."

She squared her shoulders. The guilt slid away. She'd thrown up her oh-so-familiar Sara barriers so fast it made him breathless. He was entitled to some asshole commentary.

"It's fine. I take a low-dose pill now. It's safer than it used to be," she said, her voice sounding defeated, which he hated.

But he'd come here with one goal in mind. Since he'd sidestepped her unique form of distraction well enough, he decided he'd best plunge right into it. Keeping his distance, he crossed his arms and forced himself to sound firm.

"That's my daughter in your house, and I want to be a part of her life. If you want me to fuck you now and then to take your edge off, that's fine, too. But I'll be damned if you keep me from her."

She glared at him, which in some perverse way was a relief. A pissed-off-at-him Sara he could handle. He'd said his piece, repeatedly. He didn't seek instant physical gratification at every turn anymore. And he knew what he damn well wanted. Problem was, it stood right in front of him in a five foot four, sexy, smart, frustrating and stubborn package.

Then say that, lame ass. Tell her what's in your mind right now and be done with all this posturing and bullshit.

"Fine. You can have Tuesday and Thursday nights."

"And weekends." He kept his voice calm. Negotiation was one of his many strong suits. And it distracted him from the yammering in his brain about him being as bad as she was when it came to admitting feelings. Which was why they were here, mouthing words neither of them meant, but mouthing them anyway.

He watched her jaw clench. It took everything he had not to reach out, to run his finger across it, ease her, the way he was meant to. He took a step backwards.

"Listen to me, Jack. Katie is my daughter and all I know is that one of you is her father. I don't give a damn who, so as far as you are concerned, it was an immaculate conception. The man who fathered her was too concerned about winning a prize. And I won't have Katie passed between us like some kind of trophy. Period."

Her words shot daggers in his heart, but he was resolute on this. He would be a part of the girl's life. Even if he couldn't be part of Sara's the way he wanted. He kept forging ahead with his demands. "I want her to stay at my house sometimes, too. I'll fix up a room for her. It'll be fine."

"How do I explain this to her?"

"I don't give two shits how you do it. You can keep calling me an uncle or whatever you do to delude yourself about me, but I will have this." He ran his fingers through his hair, but his knees shook so hard he had to sit back down.

The look in her eyes at that moment made him more frustrated than the combined sum total of their years together. And that was saying something.

"Okay, but the whole 'fucking me to take an edge off' thing? No thanks. I won't be what you need me to be, ever. We do nothing but frustrate each other to the point of homicide. You make me better and worse all at once. And I can't take it anymore." She looked out her window, not realizing how fully she had broken his heart. "You should find someone else. Move on. You can be part of Katie's life, but you're officially out of mine."

Jack's ears started ringing. "As long as you realize you only have to tell me that once." He left before he said something colossally stupid. Something he couldn't take back.

"Wait!" He heard her call out, and he stopped, closed his eyes a moment. Then opened them and kept walking.

No. No more. I've tried enough. She's right. I gotta find something else, maybe even someone else. But in the meantime....

He smiled at the thought of Kate's face when he told her she got to decorate her room anyway she wanted. She was his daughter. He knew it. He'd make her happy. And she would love him unconditionally. That's all he needed.

Sara slammed the door shut behind him. God damn the man to hell and back. How did he do it? Bring her such exquisite ecstasy and bone-grinding frustration within minutes. His possessiveness had obviously translated over to her daughter now and while part of her wanted it—craved it even—a bigger part of her resisted it, hard. So hard, in fact, she feared she might have just alienated him forever with a simple turn of phrase.

She grabbed her phone and quickly dialed Julie.

"Hurry, tell me not to go after him," she said as soon as her friend answered the phone.

"You know my stance on Jack. And it involves chasing him down, tackling and hog tying him before it's too late." Sara sighed and took a breath, reliving the near-miss physical connection, and the ugly words they'd thrown at each other.

"I think Katie's getting sick. You headed home soon?"

"Yeah, she got sunburned in Florida and has been sniffly and stuff since. I'm coming."

"Congratulate me."

Sara answered automatically. "Congratulations."

"I'm pregnant."

"Holy shit Julie, really? I mean. Yay." She sat. She'd just planned and implemented a sort of surprise wedding for Julie and Evan a few weeks prior. They'd seemed so happy there. Sara had seethed with jealousy during the whole thing—happy but at the same time not. She'd avoided Jack all night during the event. But this bit of news did not sound as great for her friend as it should have .

"Yeah. He's not too thrilled."

"I'm sorry Julie. That sucks."

"I made him leave, actually. Told him he could move out if he felt that strongly against having a family with me."

"Honey!" Her own troubles suddenly seemed trivial. She had a healthy, beautiful daughter. A man she loved wanting to be the girl's father. What was her fucking problem, anyway? "I'll be home in a few. And I'll drink your share of wine for you."

Unable to resist, needing to talk to him and reluctant to admit it, she dialed Jack next. "Where is he?"

"Who?"

"Your asshole friend, that's who."

"Ah, yes, you are Julie's BFF these days, aren't you?"

"What is his problem?"

"Sara, the very last thing on the planet that you and I need to be doing is projecting their relationship. They have their issues. We have ours. Let's keep them separate, shall we?"

"Whatever. Go talk some sense into him, would you? She's at my house right now."

Jack heaved a teenager-worthy sigh. "Yes, m'am," he said before he hung up.

Chapter Fifteen

Jack's head pounded. At that moment, he'd give a million of his own dollars not to be manager of a successful real estate company. The stress was going to kill him. But he smiled, remembering today was the day he and Katie were going to pick out paint and all the furnishings for her room at his house.

He pulled into Sara's driveway, noting her car in the garage. After grabbing her mail from the box, he pushed open her front door. His heart already felt lighter at the thought of an entire weekend with Katie. He'd even passed on a hot date with little thought.

He paused, taking in Sara's compact, tidy world around him. A hot date with some random woman wasn't what he wanted. He pressed his fists down on her granite counters and counted to ten, took a deep breath, refocused on why he was here. Besides, he'd had a few dates already, and had damn well enjoyed himself. He was, as she'd insisted he do, moving on. He pushed himself away from the counter.

"Sara! Katie! Where is everybody?" The house was quiet. He stuck his head in the miniscule downstairs room that passed for Sara's office and came to a dead stop. The late afternoon light shone through the window and hit her hair, lighting it up with golds and ambers. She had earbuds in her ears, and he saw the budget spreadsheets on her computer.

His chest tightened as he watched her brow furrow in concentration. His palms itched to touch her as she stretched her arms up, arching her back. God help him, he still loved her and would never stop. He smiled when she turned and jumped at the sight of him, pulling the music out of her ears.

"How long have you been...?"

"Long enough." He grinned and stood in front of her, ran a finger down her face. She moved away from him.

"Cut it out."

He shrugged, letting himself fall back into familiar territory. "Where is she?"

Sara waved her hand. "Outside, in the tree house. We had a fight, and she's pouting."

"Fight about what?"

"She wanted to make brownies the second she got the idea in her head. I needed to get some work done and told her to give me an hour. She didn't care for the delay. It devolved from there." Sara ran a hand over her face. "I'm a bad mommy, I guess."

"Nah." He kissed her cheek, not committing to anything more lest he get himself in trouble. He was trying to swear off Sara. To see how he might manage without her in his life. So far, it sucked. But he was still trying.

He strolled outside and over to the elaborate tree house Sara's brother had built last year, climbed up the ladder, and stuck his head through the floor. "Hey lovely lady. Time to go shop... Katie?"

He looked around. The space was empty. Even her favorite toys and books were gone. A small finger of panic flickered through his brain. He climbed down, determined to remain calm. He looked around both sides of the house, ran back in and up to her room, ignoring Sara's wide-eyed stare.

"Katie! Answer me now!"

She wasn't under the bed, or in any kitchen cabinets. He pushed Sara aside to stomp down to the basement. Katie didn't like basements, but she might be just stubborn enough to hide there to make a point.

"God damn it Kate, where are you?" He bounded up the steps.

"Are there any other hiding places? Any place you can think of she'd go? The park? Where?" His throat had closed up and red tinged the edges of his vision. A calm descended even as he sensed Sara's abject terror swirling around him. "Listen to me. Think. Be calm and focus." He led her to the chair and made her sit.

Tears started pouring down her face. Jack bit back the renewed urge to shake her and sat on the ottoman, gripping her ice-cold hands.

"J-j-jack. Oh God. Where is she? I'm... we. Oh shit. I did this."

"Stop it. Stop making this about you, damn it."

He stood, unable to sit for another minute, whipped out his phone and held back his own version of terror, fighting off the images of her lifted from the sidewalk by some predator. He had to keep it together.

He gazed out onto the innocent looking front lawn, the beautiful day a mere half hour before, now a nightmare. "Call your brother," he said. "I'm going to check around the neighborhood."

An hour later, he returned, sweaty under his dress shirt, finding it hard to breathe. Several cars now lined the street outside Sara's house. He shoved the door open onto the tableau. Julie sat with her arm around Sara. Evan stood at the window. Blake and Rob had their phones to their ears, shoulder to shoulder. Jack took a breath and entered the fray.

They all looked up at him. The hope on Sara's face almost undid him. "Call the police."

"Already did," Rob said. Jack stomped into the kitchen and slammed a glass of water when a sound from behind made him turn.

"Your best bet is to stay away from me right now," he said before turning to look at Sara, a complex roil of emotions churning through him: anger, frustration, need—none of it good. But he grabbed her, held on for dear life, tried to summon what he had left to give her. She clutched at his shirt. "Baby. Shh. It's okay. She's fine."

"G-g-god Jack. I was such a bitch. I told her..." She sucked in a breath. "I told her if she thought you could do it better to go live with you."

His heart pounded in his chest. "You told her what?"

"I told her to..."

He took the four steps between the kitchen and the living room in two. "Get in your car," he barked at Evan. "Go to my place via Stadium.

I'm going via downtown. Meet at Cambridge." He named his street, his head spinning, trying not to picture how many major roads the girl would have to cross to get where she was going.

"Jack, she wouldn't do that. She doesn't know how to get to your house from here." Julie had one arm around Sara.

"If she gets it in her head, she'll try. She has her phone with GPS, right? I showed her how to use it a few days ago when we were at the park. Let's go people. Blake, you stay here. Sara, come with me." Everyone scurried around and did as they were told.

Evan put a hand on his arm as he got into his SUV. "It'll be okay." Jack ignored him. Holding it together took every ounce of energy he had.

"Help me find her, okay?" He tried to keep the fear out of his voice. Sara climbed into the passenger's seat and they took off.

Sara's world had narrowed to a pinprick, a brief millisecond of time between then and now. A tiny, shiny moment where she'd stared at her own daughter and had yelled at her. The girl had been unbearable since returning from Florida. It was "Uncle Jack" twenty-four seven.

She'd had a shit day, needed to decompress, needed space. But Katie had started in on the brownies, on how she wanted them. She'd snapped and yelled at the girl. She didn't even remember what she had said until the second she recalled advising her to go live with Uncle Jack if he was so damn great. The girl's eyes had filled with tears before she stomped out.

"I hate you Mommy! I only love Uncle Jack."

Please, God, don't let those be the last words I ever hear from her. Please. Please. Please.

"Hold it together, Sara. No falling apart. Not now." Jack's voice permeated her fog of agony. "I mean it." His hand clutched her thigh. She stared at it, unable to speak. She nodded and strained her eyes left and right, begging every higher power she could conjure to catch a glimpse of the pink and purple-clad form, pulling the wagon Blake had discovered missing from the garage.

They drove slowly through downtown, leaning forward, not speaking. At South University, they had to stop and make room for a couple of screaming Ann Arbor police cars. Sara clutched Jack's leg. "Oh God."

"Stop it," he whispered. "Just don't."

The cars made their way onto Washtenaw Avenue, a busy four-lane street, and continued on, lights and sirens blaring. Jack followed them, his face grim. Sara couldn't halt the constant flow of tears. The cops pulled into the Whole Foods parking lot and screeched to a halt by the front door. Jack followed them, parked and got out. Sara didn't move until he motioned for her, his blue eyes angry. She took a breath and climbed out.

The police officers headed into the store. Jack stayed behind them. As Sara watched, he dropped to his knees right in the grocery store foyer. Her mind couldn't process it. Did he fall? The small pink and purple something that hurtled into his arms made her stumble, gasp, cry out.

"Katie!" she screeched, pushing past the gawping crowd. "Katie!" She dropped to her knees, wrapped her arms around them both. The girl seemed no worse for wear. A young couple stood behind her, talking to the police.

A hand on her face made her look up into a pair of worried green eyes. "Mommy? Mommy, are you okay?"

"I am now," Sara mumbled into her daughter's hair. Fury surged through her. She took Katie's arms, shook her. "Don't you ever, ever, ever do that again. Do you understand me? Do you hear me?" Katie started to cry in earnest.

Jack picked the sobbing girl up and, without a glance in Sara's direction, walked outside with her, leaving Sara on her knees, in the middle of the foyer, surrounded by tsk-tsk'ing parents all judging her.

She flopped onto her butt and sat, not giving a shit who had to walk around her, until a young police officer with a kind face pulled her to her feet.

Within minutes, Julie, Blake, Rob and Evan were there. Jack stayed apart, Katie cradled against him. Evan walked over to him before returning to the group. "C'mon." He tugged Sara towards his car. "I'm taking you home."

She jerked out of his grip and marched over to her daughter and put a hand on the girl's back. Jack stared at her. Katie wouldn't raise her face from his shoulder. The evening had settled in on them, purple, cool and pleasant.

"Talk to your mommy, sweetie," he muttered at her. Katie raised a tear-stained face, reached out and pulled Sara close, forcing her to hold on to Jack as well. They stood there for a while before Jack spoke.

"Katie. What did you think you were doing? Why did you leave your house?"

"I wanted to live with you. So I packed my stuff and left. I was almost there, too." Sara felt Jack shaking. She tightened her grip. "Then those people found me and made me come inside the grocery store. I was afraid of them. They're strangers. Then some police cars came. Then you got here."

Jack pulled away from Sara, leaving her alone on the sidewalk. He deposited the girl in the now permanent child seat in his SUV, shut the door and turned to her. "So help me, Sara. If you ever pull this shit again..."

"Me?"

"Yes. You. A fucking kitten has a better mother than Katie does." Sara took a step back. He closed the gap she'd created.

Blake started to say something, but Rob put a hand on his arm. Evan cleared his throat and Julie put an arm around her. Jack ducked into his car without another word to anyone and left her standing there, surrounded by her friends, his friends, and her family.

No one said a word.

Sara cried herself to sleep, her dreams a muddle of images between Jack yelling at her and Katie crying and a weird alarm that wouldn't stop clanging. She fought to be awake and saw her phone screen. Jack. Calling her at two a.m.

"What do you want?"

"Katie's sick."

"So, you're perfect. You heal her." But she was already up, getting into her clothes.

"She's burning up and crying about her ears."

"Ear infection. Give her some Tylenol and I'll take her to the pediatrician tomorrow."

"I'm going to the ER now. Meet me there if you want." The phone went dead.

Great. Yet one more example of her as shit mom of the year. Maybe she should let Jack raise the kid. Her face got hot.

Fuck that. I carried her. I birthed her. I nursed and raised her. Fuck him and his self-righteousness.

She grabbed her keys and purse and ran to her car.

Once there, she heard the girl's wails of agony emanating from a curtained-off area. They were interspersed with a familiar sound. One Sara recognized as Katie's drama queen voice.

She shoved past the angry-looking nurses and yanked open a curtain revealing her daughter, in her Disney princess pj's, crying her eyes out while the attending doctor tried to look in her ears. Jack stood to one side, looking pale and helpless.

Sara scooped the girl into her arms.

"Mommy!" she wailed. Sara ignored everyone around her and held her daughter close.

Later, after a healthy dose of antibiotics and pain killers the girl slept against Sara's shoulder. They were still stuck in the ER since the doctors didn't want to release her until her fever came down.

"I'm sorry," Jack muttered from his position in the chair next to her.

"It's fine." She spoke into the girl's sweaty hair so she didn't have to look at him. "It's not as easy as you think. Okay? Stop making me the bad guy. You have no idea what I've gone through with her for the last almost five years."

Jack slid onto the hard, uncomfortable bed alongside her. Sara tried to stay mad, but his arms went around her. His lips touched her ear. "I'm so sorry, Sara. You are a great mom. I'm such a shit. But I..." He stopped and sucked in a breath. "I just pictured her, you know.... Never mind."

Sara took a deep breath. "I love you."

Jack sighed, and the sound made her close her eyes against the inevitable. "Afraid it's too little too late. You can only push me away so many times until I get the message. And I got it. Loud and clear." He kissed her hair and got up.

She closed her eyes and felt a tear slip down her cheek.

Too little. Too late. The story of her life.

"You should take her home. I'll call you tomorrow." He leaned down to kiss Katie's cheek, then walked out of the room. And her life, she supposed, but for the co-parenting thing.

The sob broke through before she could stop it.

"Mommy?" Katie's small hand touched her face. "Mommy, why are you crying? I'm sorry."

"No, no, baby, it's not you. Don't worry." She kissed her daughter's flushed cheek.

"Where's Uncle Jack?" The girl snuggled in closer. Sara shifted, trying to find a comfortable position on the rock hard emergency room bed. She figured she was stuck here for a while, anyway.

"He had to go, baby."

She slept, she thought. Or at least she dozed as much as possible, sitting mostly upright and surrounded by a busy emergency department. When a warm hand touched her shoulder, she flinched.

"Jack?" she said, wishing him back. Knowing he wouldn't be back. Not anymore. And that was one hundred percent her fault.

"Let's get you guys home," Blake said.

Chapter Sixteen

"No, Mom, you don't have to do anything." Sara's mind was half on the conversation and half on the crisis unfolding with one of her newest agents. The guy had flat out forgotten to sign a buyer's agency agreement again, and was now moaning that some people he'd been hauling all over, looking at houses, bought from a seller's agent at an open house.

She read the latest email from him, begging for her help. "I gotta go. I'll see you and Dad tomorrow night at the party. How long are you staying?" She winced at the answer. "Sure, great. Yeah, Julie and I planned the whole thing. I think we're good to go."

Within minutes, the agent in question appeared at her door. Tall, nervous-looking, with an air of resigned desperation, he represented one of her first bad calls when it came to taking on new agents. Handsome, as required of the downtown sales people, but with nothing much behind the pretty face. She sighed and pointed to the seat opposite her desk.

"Okay, so unfortunately you don't have a leg to stand on." He started to protest, but she cut him off. "But don't worry. I blame myself and bad training." She leaned her elbows on her desk. "Always sign the buyer's agency, David. This is your mulligan, okay?" The guy left without a word.

She flopped back in her chair, frustration coursing through her. It had been a hell of a day, and it wasn't about to be over anytime soon. Katie's seven-year-old birthday party was tonight and all forty invitees were arriving soon. There was a giant bouncy castle, a zillion white lights in her trees, a tent, Blake and Rob in charge of food for everyone, and booze for the parents. The weather promised to be brutally hot, just like the day Katie had been born. The bonus of her parents' presence promised a new level of stress.

The endless arguments with her father for the last seven years and nine months, his harping on her decision to keep both men out of her life for so long, had turned on its ear. Now that Jack was around, her father couldn't stand it.

Jesus. She couldn't win.

Keeping Jack at arm's length, their only actual communication terse and clipped, as if they'd skipped marriage and gone straight to being a grumpy divorced couple, was taking its toll on her too, making her tense and snappish and exhausted.

Julie interrupted her pity party with a call. "I'm headed to your place. The girls are sleeping in the car now, but will be ready to party later. Your brother has the food and stuff sorted, right?"

"Yeah."

"What's wrong?"

"Sorry. Nothing."

"He'll be there?"

"Yes."

"And you have what you need for later?"

"I suppose."

"Don't you dare chicken out now, Sara. I mean it. I got Evan back. Now I am bound and determined that you and Jack figure yourselves out."

"Whatever." Sara turned onto her street and sighed at the sight of her father's Caddy in her driveway alongside Jack's Corvette. "See you in a few."

She sat in the car a minute, letting her mind wander, remembering the moment about a year ago that she and Jack had breached the wall she'd thrown up between them.

• • • •

SARA WAS AT WORK LATE, on a summer evening while Katie was with a sitter, buried in sales forecasts and the infernal budgeting Jack insisted on. Her phone rang three times in a row after she ignored it, unwilling to hear any more from Jack about whatever crawled up his ass regarding her latest proposal.

"Where the hell is Kate?" He yelled into her ear. He'd adopted a shortened version of her already short nickname. "Uncle Jack" called her Kate. No one else did. Sara was speechless, her brain attempting to process that question.

"What..."

Jack cut her off. "She just called me Sara, from inside the track at Pioneer." He named the high school that lay a solid ten blocks from her house. "She rode her bike, climbed the fence and now can't get out. Goddamn it, I told you I didn't trust that sitter. Has she even noticed? Fuck! Never mind, I'm on my way there now."

"We had a fight this morning." Sara slumped into her chair. "She... she told me she wanted to live with you all the time." The parallels to the moment two years prior, when the girl had marched herself nearly three miles from their home to find his house, thrummed in her ears.

That moment had been a turning point. One that made Sara realize that perhaps being with Jack wasn't the answer.

"I never suggested that to her. You know I don't spoil her. She eats healthy, gets plenty of sleep, I..."

Sara ran a hand down her face. "I know."

Katie's infernal ability to provoke her escalated, and the last words out of the girl's mouth as Sara shut the door were, "You're terrible, mean, and I hate you!"

"You should go," Jack said, his voice quiet. "If it's an issue between you two, I shouldn't get in the middle. I don't want her to consider me her rescue option."

"Why are you so fucking logical?"

He laughed, and the iceberg around her heart cracked ever so slightly. She spoke without thinking.

"I miss you."

The silence on his end stretched out. She grabbed her keys and headed to the door.

"Let's talk more after you get her. Tell her next time Uncle Jack says if she can climb over the fence to get in, she can climb over and get out."

"Okay. Thank you."

"No problem."

After that, they eased into a wary friendship-slash-truce, and the entire Stewart Real Estate Company rejoiced. It meant fewer fraught upper management meetings. Jack Gordon was a hard-ass leader, tough, firm, driven and with high expectations of everyone around him. He'd turned the brokerage around. But for the past year and a half, he'd been impossible to work with. His antsy, quick temper exacerbated by proximity to Sara. He hardly left the office even to sleep or eat except on Tuesdays and Thursdays—the days he had Kate at his house.

They'd returned to nighttime phone conversations, lasting long into the night three or four times a week, and between sorting through work issues and discussing theories of raising a successful future woman. Recently, they'd drifted into more personal details.

"So…" she'd asked at one point, needing to know but dreading the answer at the same time. "Have you, um, moved on, like I told you to?"

"Since when do I do what you tell me?"

She'd shivered at the sound of his voice. It compelled her in so many ways, for good and bad. She needed to hear it, like she needed to drink water.

"Never mind."

"And you? Find a new boyfriend yet?"

"Yeah, in all my spare time, I'm out clubbing, picking up randoms."

"Well, there is the internet."

"No thanks. You gonna answer me?"

He sighed. "I've been out on a few dates."

"Well, that's good."

"Oh shut up. You're jealous."

"Yeah, I am." She sighed. "We sure are good at bad timing, aren't we?"

"You, my dear, are the queen of overreaction. But I still love you."

Her scalp had tingled, and she snuggled down in the covers. "Don't know why. I'm a real bitch, I hear."

He chuckled and her thighs tightened at the sound. "You horny, baby? That what this is about?"

She'd bitten her lip. "You psychic?"

"Only as relates to you."

"Good night Jack. See you tomorrow."

"Wait—let's have phone sex. It'll be fun."

It had been her turn to chuckle. "You are so..."

"Blue-balled? Seriously Sara. I may go out to keep myself from going crazy, but...I can't...oh hell, why am I telling you, anyway? You'll just gloat."

"No, I won't. Tell me."

"Another time. When you're on your knees, begging me."

"Dream on."

"No, you will be."

She'd shuddered, her whole body on fire now with the need for his hands, his lips, his voice. "Stop it."

"I'm not doing anything."

She'd sighed, realizing the hopelessness of her entire relationship with him.

• • • •

BY THE TIME SHE GOT home, Katie was a whirling dervish of excitement. The sitter looked harried as she relayed the afternoon's events.

"She's changed outfits three times and was obsessing over how to keep two of her favorite men — Uncle Jack and Grandpa — from ruining her party with arguments." The young woman grabbed her bag, eager to escape.

"Just make sure he has his whiskey. Mama," the girl advised, as she sat up on the counter and watched Sara making coffee. "He'll be okay then."

Sara laughed and patted the girl's knee. "You're almost too big to sit there. And who gets the whiskey? Grandpa or Uncle Jack?"

"Grandpa. Definitely. Uncle Jack doesn't drink that much anymore." She raised an eyebrow at her mother, making Sara bite down on the urge to remind Katie she'd known her Uncle Jack a lot longer. But gave up, realizing it was petty and would only lead to a fight. The girl ran for the door to meet her Uncle Rob with a huge hug.

"Princess!" Rob hauled her up onto his shoulders. The girl had all the men in her life wrapped around her grubby little finger. If she was honest with herself, she admired Katie even more for it. "I have your birthday feast. The one you requested. Want to help me set it up?"

"Yes! Yes! I'll help."

He winked at Sara and took the chattering, over stimulated girl outside.

Sara sipped her coffee and watched the as the bouncy castle inflated. The tent was already up, tables, plates, utensils set out by Blake and Rob's catering staff.

Katie danced around from person to person, running her mouth. Every adult in the place was in the palm of her hand within minutes. The girl knew no strangers. She wore her heart on her sleeve, twenty-four seven. You never had to wonder what was on her mind. Sara marveled at it, remembering her own guarded personality, even as a child.

Sara smiled, watching her. Katie's hair had darkened to a deep chestnut brown. Her long, sturdy legs flashed under the crazy purple skirt she'd chosen. Sara's eyes skipped over the backyard. Julie sat holding one of her baby girls, Evan the other. The twins were a surprise, and a double handful. But Evan took to his new role as dad like a pro. Her friend smiled at her.

Katie tugged at her sleeve. "Mommy! Can I go to Jason's next week? He wants me over for a play date."

"Only on Fridays, remember?"

The girl's week had a regimen born of busy parents and her own commitments. Sara made Jack promise to handle all aspects of the new soccer thing he'd gotten her into. But she wasn't oblivious to the potential the coaches already saw in her daughter and figured she'd be in for some bleacher time soon enough.

Sara finished her coffee and wandered out onto the patio. The bar was set up. Everything was ready to go. The doorbell rang.

It starts.

Wishing she'd reached for alcohol instead of caffeine, Sara squared her shoulders and opened the door to find a man she hadn't seen in over a year standing there, lopsided grin and all. His deep brown eyes and still too-long blonde hair had not changed a bit, but an attractive light red beard covered his jaw.

She put a hand over her mouth.

Craig gathered her in his arms and held her close. She closed her eyes and melted into his embrace, ignoring her father's smug face.

Craig had forgotten how much he loved having Sara in his arms.

"You're here." Sara's voice was muffled against his chest.

"Uncle Craig!" The squeal of delight made him release Sara and look across the yard. The girl ran straight for him. He frowned and glanced up at Sara. She smiled at him while accepting a beer from Blake. Katie launched into his arms, and he spun her around, thrilled and shocked at how much she'd changed in a year.

"C'mon, let's bounce!" She took his hand and let her lead him to the castle, already teeming with small bodies.

"You go ahead, honey, I'll watch."

Katie shrugged and climbed in, joining the fray of squealing participants.

"Craig," Jack said. He'd gone a little grey at the temples but otherwise looked the same: tall, handsome, confident, and comfortable in a pair of dark jeans and a polo shirt. "Good to see you. In for a few days?"

"Ah, no. Moving back and joining a practice."

Jack narrowed his eyes, but slapped him on the shoulder. "Of course you are. Can't keep things simple around here too long, can we?" The two men smiled at each other and walked towards Sara and her parents, still standing up on the patio.

Chapter Seventeen

After a couple of hours, Sara thought her head would explode from noise and stress. She and Julie had planned it all out, but the actual implementation took a ton of energy.

"He's quite the success, isn't he?" Her father walked up to her as she took a breather from the kids.

"Who?"

Matthew pointed over to Craig, who stood admiring Julie's twin girls.

"Sure. I guess."

"Would be quite a catch, I'd say."

Sara turned to her mother. "Keep him away from me or I'm gonna kick him out."

Blake walked up holding a plateful of food. "How in the hell did all that get eaten? My god we brought enough food to feed an adult army battalion."

She glanced at him, then dashed over to defuse some kind of seven-year-old ruckus near the water balloons. "Do me a solid? The next time I use 'water balloons' and 'birthday party' in the same sentence, slap duct tape over my mouth," she tossed over her shoulder.

She saw Jack emerge from the bouncy castle, a little green around the gills. The few parents who hadn't stuck around for the free food and booze started showing up, took one look at the chaos and started eyeballing Sara as if she were an evil stepmother.

Katie sat nestled in a group of her soccer and school friends, ripping paper from gifts without even noticing what they were. Sara caught Jack's eye over the heads of the crowd, hoping like hell he got the message to shut the thing down.

He did. Plucking Katie up and perching her on his shoulders, he let a few kids latch onto his legs and he walked the whole crowd over the patio like a tall, handsome Pied Piper. Sara smiled and turned to some mom who'd just appeared at her elbow, bitching about gluten-free cake and tree nut allergies.

It took a grand total of twenty minutes to divest her backyard of thirty-eight small, over-stimulated kids. Which left her immediate family and close friends. She headed toward Jack. "A little over the top, wouldn't you say Gordon? The girl is only seven after all," her father was saying.

Katie had climbed up into Jack's lap and fallen asleep, draped over his shoulder. He kept a hand on her back. The other gripped a glass of bourbon. Sara shot him a look from behind Matthew's, with what she hoped was a clear, "Don't engage. It's not worth it," message.

He grinned and winked at her. "Yeah, maybe. But a damn good time. Glad you could make it, Matt." Sara blew him a kiss.

Julie's question ghosted through her brain. She'd confided in her friend last week. When told she'd been determined to win him back, to convince him she was serious about them as a couple, the three of them as a family, Julie had said that it would be up to her. That she had to open up and admit it to him. To make herself as vulnerable as he had the two times he'd asked her to marry him. Sara gulped, thinking of the small package she had hidden in her bedside table for later. But the surprise arrival of Craig had thrown her off. Just as she was thinking of him, he put an arm around her waist and kissed her cheek.

She smiled and turned to him. "You look great. I like this." She ran her finger down his bearded jaw. "Sexy and rugged. Congrats on the ER thing."

"I always planned to come back here. I hadn't figured out how, but..." He shrugged and took a drink of his beer. They stood, watching Blake and Rob relax together in her hammock. "Those two okay?"

She leaned into him. "Yeah, thank God. They're talking about adopting, but Blake doesn't want to." Sara relished Craig's way of putting her at ease, no matter what.

"I'd think he would be the one advocating for it. He's always been so great with Katie."

"Yeah, he wants a biological child using a surrogate."

"Ah. Complicated."

"Yeah. But, in an even more bizarre twist, Rob told me he thought they should take it even one more step. Find a woman to share their lives."

"I understand you can get those on the internet." His voice was serious. She looked up at his twinkling brown eyes and her heart did a little dance in her chest.

She punched his shoulder. "Be nice."

He laughed and pulled her into an embrace. "It's so good to see you. To see her. She's amazing. You've... you and Jack... have done a great job."

Sara sucked in a deep breath, keeping her nose buried in his shirtfront. "Thanks. But it's likely more him than me."

She looked up at him, keeping her hands clasped behind his waist. The eyes of the patio were on them, she knew, but she didn't care. He touched her cheek.

"I asked Suzanne to marry me yesterday." Sara blinked, released him, and ran her hand up her chilled arm.

"Oh. Well, double congratulations."

She tried to force down the irrational jealousy that poked her consciousness.

I let him go. Can't blame him for moving on.

But with Suzanne?

"She said no." Her eyes flew open. Sara tried to gauge his state of mind, but his face stayed neutral. "Told me I had to get you out of my system first. Said she wouldn't play understudy." He sighed, and Sara realized how tired he looked.

"I've screwed up your life, too? Wow! I am on a roll."

Rob and Blake interrupted before he responded, walking up and taking over the conversation with Craig. "Excuse me," she stepped back, "I need to..." she let the words fade as she escaped, already questioning her decision about tonight.

Chapter Eighteen

"Dear Lord. I feel like I've been beaten up by a biker gang," Jack groaned from the living room. All the guests had dispersed, and Katie was passed out in her bed. Sara puttered around in the kitchen, nervous energy making her heart fluttery. Visions of Craig, images of his face when he saw how Katie had changed and seemed to be morphing into a blend of him and her, and his words, "She said no," clanged around in her brain.

"Hey, bring me some alcohol." His deep voice made her smile. She poured them each a glass of wine, pictured the small flat box she had tucked into the side table drawer. It calmed her.

The long conversations she'd had with Julie about that woman's decision to bind herself to Evan this way first, before they married, had made an enormous impact. Sara wanted to convince Jack she meant this—that she wanted them to be together. They had an awful lot of bullshit behind them. And she wasn't a hundred percent sure that wearing some kind of expensive necklace made the sort of statement that mattered to him anymore. But she was willing to give it a shot.

She wandered back into the living room. She'd turned this space into her oasis. Clean, neutral walls, mostly cream and brown furnishings; she'd discovered that sitting here soothed her with its simplicity. Jack sat on her soft white rug, legs sprawled out, head leaning back against the couch. He still was breathtaking, even with a sprinkling of grey in his thick hair.

She joined him, curling her legs under her. They clinked glasses.

"Nice party, Sara. Well done."

"You'd think it would be easy to impress a bunch of seven-year-olds. I assure you it is not." She laughed and sipped, keeping her eyes averted, still wondering if this whole scenario she'd cooked up would be a huge mistake.

He kept an arm draped around her shoulder, traced circles on her bare shoulder with a finger while he sipped. "Good to see Craig. Seems he's gonna be a more permanent fixture around here... again."

"Yeah." She wondered how her life could get so complicated, just as she'd decided what she wanted.

Jack. She wanted Jack.

She had to do it before she backed out. She'd waited long enough.

Jaw set, she stood.

"Where ya going?" He tugged her down, pressed her back onto the thick rug. She looked up at him. He had his arms on either side of her and leaned down, brushing his lips against hers. "Stay," he whispered.

"Okay, but I have..." He cut her off with a kiss so fierce, so intense, it made her dizzy. His tongue swept into her mouth, lips firm against hers. He intoxicated her and brought her release all at once. She put her feet on the floor, needing something solid, something to assure herself she hadn't floated away on a cloud of desire from the mere touch of his mouth on hers. She broke away.

"Wow. What was that for? Not that I'm complaining."

He grinned, making his eyes sparkle, which sent her insides into their usual Jack-induced meltdown. He ran a finger down her face. The look in his eyes alarmed her—it contained regret, and very little hope.

She propped up on her elbows. "What? Really, Jack, why did you do that? We haven't touched each other in two years. Why now?"

"Because you needed it."

She made a frustrated sound and looked away from him. He pushed her back onto the rug again in one swift movement and pinned her hands over her head. She struggled against him. Her earlier resolve had vanished. Confusion flooded her brain. But her body thrummed, recognizing and loving his power over her.

"I did not."

"You did too."

"Not."

"Too. Look at me Sara."

She turned her face to his, eager, and yet nervous about how easy this all was tonight.

He possessed her mouth once more, ran a hand down her breast, flicked her nipple while keeping her wrists still under his grasp. She shifted, wrapped a leg around his waist. His need pressed against her body and she arched into it, her world once again a swirl of dark emotion—a darkness she let herself own.

His hand slipped inside her shorts. Sara sighed neck as her long-neglected body fielded its first true release since... well, since the last time she'd been with him. He teased her clit, pressed fingers high into her, making her bite down on a squeal of pleasure. "May I? Please?"

He stopped, still as a stone, lips hovering over hers. His tongue flicked out, touched her lips. "Yes." The one simple word, whispered deep in his throat, made her ears go quiet, shut out all sensation but his lips and fingers.

"That's it baby. Give it to me. All of it." He kept up the monologue, anchoring her as his fingers stoked her, making her quiver, moan, want more.

"Give me your heart, Sara, please." He nuzzled her neck. "I'll take care of it for you, I promise." She gasped.

"Might be tough, considering you're still dressed." She grinned at him as he jumped up and stripped out of his jeans and polo shirt in two seconds flat. He tugged her shorts down and off, yanked her shirt up and off, freeing her breasts with a flick of his fingers.

He was over her in a heartbeat, reaching over her head and threading his long fingers through her, kissing her until she saw stars. With a shift of his hips, he entered her body and soul with one decisive movement.

Wrapping both legs around his waist, she held him still, looked in his eyes as he moved his hips, reaching up high. She tightened all her muscles.

"Kiss me, Jack," she whispered.

He did, giving her what she needed. Then tilted his hips, gasping into her lips as he shuddered with his own release. She sighed, stretched beneath him, traced his lips with her tongue.

"You'll take care of my heart, eh?"

He groaned, slipped out of her, and collapsed on the rug beside her.

"I will. Although I guess you can call me the goddamned ten-second man, sorry. Jesus." He ran a shaking hand over his face. She grinned and went up on an elbow. "You know how to make a man pent up."

"I didn't do that. You did. You can't tell me there isn't a line of women at your door willing to take your edge off." She stood, tugged her shorts back on, and grabbed her wine. "Whatever, I'm kidding. I have something for you. It's in my room. Give me a sec." She pulled the large, flat velvet box from the drawer and arranged herself on the bed. Unsure how to present it, she sat on the edge of her bed, holding it in her lap.

She heard him get a drink of water, then climb the steps. The gasp when she opened the box sounded serious. He took the few steps to her bed and shut it, then tossed it to the floor.

"No, Sara, that's not what we're about." He kissed her, hard. When he released her, he plucked the box from the floor, opened it and pulled the thin platinum choker from it, turning it in his hands. She swallowed hard.

"I thought, I mean... I wanted to make a statement about... us."

"I get it. I did the same thing about eight years ago, at a large sales meeting?" She looked away. "But this, while appreciated, isn't necessary. I don't want you that way."

She stood, anger replacing nervousness. "How exactly do you want me?"

"As an equal. I don't want there to be any confusion about that."

"But this isn't about equality, right? It's about trust. I'm trying to tell you, Jack, I trust you. Trust you enough to wear this so the entire world knows." A whimper from upstairs made them both look up. Sara sighed as he kissed her nose.

"It's too much, too soon. Kinda like that first time I proposed, okay? We need to get our heads around all of this. You and me both." He made for the door now that the sounds materialized into a coherent cry for Uncle Jack.

"But..." She followed him out and stood at the steps, listening as he soothed Katie, got her a drink of water and shut the door behind him. He took a seat on the bottom stair, tugged her down alongside him.

"Can I be honest?"

She nodded and leaned against his shoulder.

"That first time. I... I wasn't ready for marriage. I was making a statement, forcing you into something neither of us was prepared for. You figured it out and most likely saved us from an expensive divorce." She wanted to protest, but he put a finger over her mouth. "I've done a shitload of soul searching on this. As hard as it is for me to admit, and as much as I love you, I think we need more time."

She watched, incredulous, as the man who'd begged her to marry him repeatedly, started for the front door after she'd offered him what she thought was something even deeper.

The door shut, and she was alone. She sat, trying to process it, trying to will away the knee-jerk reaction that resembled anger. He had a point. She turned his words over in her head, trying to find solace, or hope. She wanted nothing more than a life with him and was ready to admit it. She thought she'd done the right thing. But he'd rejected her.

She gasped and covered her mouth as the truth of this moment bowled her over. Now, she understood how he felt all those times he'd asked her to marry him and she'd blown him off, casual and breezy. Now she got it.

The crystal vase made a very satisfying crash against the wall. The water and ruined flowers soaked the drywall, but didn't stop the pounding in her head, repeating the words "as much as I love you" repeatedly.

Julie answered right away. "How did it go?" Sara could hear the girls fussing in the background.

"Not well."

"What? Hang on a sec. Evan! Can you please... thanks. Now, what did he say?"

"He doesn't want it. He wants a partnership. Says I'm not ready for that step. Shit, I don't know anymore. Maybe it isn't meant to be." The thought of that made her nearly choke on unhappiness.

Jack sat in his car, forehead pressed to his steering wheel for a solid five minutes, trying to catch his breath. He sat up, gripped the steering wheel and touched the phone icon, grinding out "Call Evan" clearly enough for the device to obey.

"Yo, what's up?" His friend's voice soothed him. Sounds of babbling in the background made him smile.

"Hey. I just needed somebody to tell me I did the right thing just now."

"Hang on a second." He heard Evan talking to his wife, her sounds of agreement and more baby noises, while he left the room.

"Sorry," he mumbled when Evan returned.

"Dude, I needed a break. No worries. I'm hiding in my man cave as we speak, holding a double scotch and fondling a cigar. Spill it."

"She tried to... she had a... a collar. I flipped out." He put his head back against the wheel, his brain spinning.

"Jesus. Why? I mean. You've said yourself that's not the sort of relationship you want with her."

"I want a relationship with her. A permanent one. Why did I say no? Jesus."

"Because it's not right. Not yet, anyway. Although sometimes I wonder about you guys. You'll be sixty years old before you both give in and acknowledge what everybody around you already does."

"Except for her father, of course. And that damn kid who might be..."

Evan cut him off. "You're doing the right thing. Stay strong. Now, I gotta get back to my estrogen Rockettes before Julie runs screaming into the night."

"Thanks man. And tell Julie if she needs a real man, my door is always open."

"Yeah, as if she'd take your sorry ass after having my magnificence."

"Oh, well, I guess I'll let her tell you."

"Fuck you Gordon."

"Julie? Anytime. Talk soon."

Chapter Nineteen

Sara let the warm breeze kicking up over Lake Michigan soothe her rattled psyche. The perfect quiet moment allowed her to reflect on why she still ached for Jack, even though she still saw him almost every day, talked to him most nights, and exchanged Katie on the regular. But it wasn't enough. She wanted more, and she'd blown it. Waited too long. Too little too late was her new mantra.

At the end of September rolled around and Blake hosted a family get together out at the cabin he and Rob had purchased up North, and Sara had never looked forward to it more. Her parents stayed at their own place two houses down the beach, but met them for lunch and dinner every day. She'd almost skipped the whole thing thanks to a lawsuit that another brokerage had threatened her office with, but Jack had convinced her to get away. He'd said he'd be up for a day himself.

Katie splashed in the cool water of the lake. Rob stood and watched, then kicked her obnoxious pink soccer ball up and down the beach with her while Blake made their evening meal. Craig was due to arrive tonight, and Sara couldn't sort out how she felt about that.

She'd stopped by Suzanne's bar once, hoping to clear the air, but the woman had been too busy to talk, or unwilling to engage with her, one or the other. Whatever hold she still had over Craig, or whatever feelings he still had for her, they had to get past it. Craig deserved happiness.

A cold bottle pressed to her bare shoulder, making her jump. Craig smiled down at her and handed her one, dropping into the chair next to her with a groan. "Christ, I'm shattered."

"I'm sure. You thought real estate was stressful?"

He chuckled. "Yeah, I love it though. I won't kid you."

"Uncle Craig!" Katie came running up and fell onto his lap.

"Katie!" Sara tried to pull her off. "Don't get him all wet and sandy."

"I don't care," he declared, burying his nose in her hair. She sat up and filled him in on every aspect of her life in about ten minutes, talking a hundred miles a minute, as usual.

Sara shut it out and sipped her beer, watching Rob kick the soccer ball around. Katie leapt up and joined him, ducking between his long legs to steal the ball and dribble it down the beach. Craig sighed and stretched out on the lounge chair.

"I heard you tried to talk to Suzanne."

She continued to ponder the lake. "Are you guys, um...?"

"No. I took her at her word. I've been working like mad, picking up extra shifts as the low man on the practice totem pole. I'm not worth more than collapsing on the couch after." He took a drink of his beer. "But I would, if she'd let me."

"I'm sorry."

"Why? It's not your fault. It's mine. C'mon, Blake told me to bring you guys up for dinner." He hauled her to her feet.

Craig held her hand later, again, as they walked down the beach. The silence stretched between them, but in a comfortable way. When they spoke, it was of innocuous things. His chest ached with longing—but for whom, he wasn't sure anymore. Finally he stopped, pulled her close. "I missed you." He ran a finger down her face.

She smiled and took his hand. "Go to Suzanne, Craig. Tell her you love her. You both deserve happiness." He dropped his hands and looked at her. The ache remained, but for someone else.

"You're right."

"Go tonight." She whirled on him. Her eyes glistened in the waning light of the late summer day. "Don't wait another minute." She bit her lip.

"I do love you Sara."

She shook her head. "No. You don't. Stop saying it. You love the idea of me. You always did. But the woman you do love is waiting for you. Make it worth her while. I know you can." She touched his lips. "I release you."

He grinned, ran his hand through his hair and took off running back up the beach. He grabbed his phone from his pocket and dashed off a quick text.

"I'm coming home tonight. Be ready for me." By the time he'd reached the cabin, he had his answer.

"I'll be waiting."

Sara sat, let a single tear fall, then took a breath and congratulated herself for the first selfless thing she'd done in a while. Even if Craig was Katie's biological father, his place in her life had been fleeting. He would remain an uncle. She sighed and sat back. The central dilemma remained.

How to convince Jack she was serious?

The sound of her name made her jump up and head back towards the steps. Anxiety ripped through her at the sound of Katie's cry. When she reached the cabin, Craig had the girl on his lap, trying to examine her foot while blood poured from a huge gash in her instep.

"What happened?" Katie was shrieking, gasping with sobs unlike her. Sara looked over at Blake. He motioned for her to come outside.

"Jack called. He's not coming."

"Well, that explains Katie's hysteria. Why not?"

Blake led her further away from the open window.

"It's his sister. She's... I guess her husband is dead." Sara gasped and ran inside for her phone. "He's already on a plane to Germany. He said he'd call you when he got there. Katie got the word and ran outside to find you. Must have stepped on a stick in the yard. Craig found her on his way back up." Blake gave her an odd look. "Craig said he had to go too."

Sara gave her brother a hug.

"Yeah, honey, he and Suzanne..." Blake sighed into her neck.

"Good. She deserves someone like him."

Sara's head pounded. She should go with Jack to help, or something. She'd only met Maureen and Brandis once, right before they moved from Colorado to the German base. But she knew how important they were to him. She walked back in to find Katie calming in Craig's arms, her foot covered with a bandage.

"She won't need stitches but has to stay out of the water and sand tomorrow, sorry."

Sara found her phone, trying Jack's number despite Blake's insistence that he couldn't be reached. The sounds of an airline staff preparing for takeoff met her ears.

"Hey. I'm glad you called." His voice was tight with tension. She ached for him, wishing she could help.

"Do you want me to come with you?"

He sighed.

"No, I'll handle it, but I don't know how long I'll be gone. You and Jason are in charge, okay?" It took her a minute to realize he meant of the real estate company. "I'll call you as soon as I land."

"I love you," she blurted into the phone, but it had already gone dead. Sighing, she pulled Katie out of Craig's lap and flopped down on the couch with her. Craig stood, pressed a kiss to hers and the girl's foreheads, and left.

Chapter Twenty

"Where the hell is it?" Sara stood at Jack's enormous desk, which was devoid of anything cluttering its rich walnut surface. His laptop docking station and huge monitor took up one corner. The only other thing she could find were business cards in a black leather holder and his heavy fountain pen—the very one she'd given him as a birthday present during the months of their brief, turbulent engagement. She smiled at it but refocused, realizing she'd need Jason to help her locate the mediation file.

Jack had stayed in Germany after his brother-in-law's funeral, helping prep his sister's family for a return to the states. Maureen was near catatonic, only just coming around long enough to cry for the bulk of each day, leaving Jack in charge of the kids, the military's paperwork machine and other details.

So, she and Jason had to handle this week's high-level mediation between one of their oldest and most respected agents, and a buyer who claimed the agent and seller had withheld crucial information about a house's plumbing system. Michigan's standard real estate purchase agreements locked all parties into an industry supervised conversation prior to anyone filing lawsuits and cases rarely went past that stage, with one party acquiescing, paying out to settle the case.

This one she wasn't so sure about. The agent in question had been one of their top producers in her day, but had lately shown signs of something close to dementia, refusing any offers of help or the not-so-subtle suggestions she retire. Sara sighed and dropped into Jack's enormous leather chair.

Her nerves were on fire from the stress of handling operations for the entire company for almost a month. She needed him here. Period. She put her head on the desk, getting a quick whiff of Jack's subtle cologne. It made her want to cry.

"Um, hi. Is Jack around?"

The soft female voice made Sara's body tense as she looked up to see one of the most shockingly attractive women she'd ever laid eyes on. She wore a slim fitting brown suit, matching pumps, had her chestnut hair in an on-purpose messy up-do. Bright blue eyes seemed confused at the sight of Sara in Jack's chair. Sara wiped a hand across her eyes, sucked in her gut and stood, never more conscious of her age. "No, he won't be back for at least another week. Can I help you? I don't think we've met."

She ought to come out from behind the desk, shake the gorgeous woman's no doubt perfectly manicured hand. But something made her stay where she was.

"I'm Shannon Simon, a new agent. I was just, um, well, never mind." The other woman's gaze flickered up and down Sara's equally well-dressed form, making her face heat up. "He told me he'd be back." A sudden piercing realization hit Sara between the eyes. She sat back down, staking her claim as best she could.

"No. His family situation is..."

"I know." The woman waved an indeed well-maintained hand. Sara bristled.

"Okay. Can I..."

"No, no. I'll call him. Thanks." The woman stayed in the doorway. Jason appeared at her elbow. Sara sensed her temper lurking around the corner, but forced it back. She had no business knowing anything about any of this.

"Sara, Jack's on line one." The model-worthy woman raised an eyebrow at her.

"Well, Shannon, so nice to meet you. Please excuse me."

"So you're Sara." The woman's gaze took on a sharp edge Sara did not care for, not one bit.

Jason rolled his eyes and pulled the woman out of the room. Sara stared at the light on the phone. Warring emotions scrabbled for her attention. She blinked when Jason reappeared in the door.

"Line one, Sara." She nodded and picked it up, closing her eyes at the sound of Jack's voice from thousands of miles away.

"Yes." She kept her voice short, busying herself by scrabbling around in his super neat files. Finding nothing related to the case, she sighed.

"You okay?" The deep growl of his voice made her shiver. She tried to remind herself what he was going through right now. But she let the jealous light blind her instead.

"No. I'm not. Where's the file?"

"Jason has the details. Notes are on my computer. Password is K-A-T-E." Sara flinched and shoved down the urge to snap at him. He'd been through so much. Maybe she'd overreacted.

No, she hadn't. She knew a predatory look in another woman's eyes when she saw it.

"Fine."

"Okay then. You'll be fine. Karen is on her last legs, at least as an agent. But there's no way she slipped like that. I have the proof."

"That's great." She sat and let the silence get uncomfortable.

"What's wrong Sara? I don't have time for bullshit. You have no idea what I'm dealing with right now." Sara heard his niece's voice in the background, shouting at her brother. Jack sighed. "Christ. This is such a mess. I... I wish had brought you with me. I could use..."

"Who the hell is Shannon?" His silence spoke volumes. "Never mind. None of my business. But did you check her ID? Just to be safe?"

"She's a new agent."

"I gathered that. What else is she, Jack?"

"That would fall under the 'none of your business' category."

"I guess, except for the fact that you and I are supposed to be working through our issues, so we might be together?"

"Honey, hang on. Uncle Jack is on the phone. Go find your mom for me, will ya?"

"Mommy won't get out of bed, Uncle Jack. Can you come?"

"Okay, I'm coming."

Sara steeled herself.

"Sara, listen, I met Shannon at... well, at the club downtown. We got to talking, ah, afterward. She'd just set a sales record at her pharma company. I talked her into changing careers."

"I get it. She's your reason for needing time to sort things out, isn't she, Jack?" Sara hated the sound of her voice, the intense feeling of raw, painful jealousy surging through her soul. "How long have you been going back to that club? The one you refuse to take me to?"

She could picture him running his long fingers through his hair, like he did whenever he got stressed. "Yes, okay. Yes. She is, but that's just part of it. You aren't sure either. That whole scene with the collar was for my benefit, not yours. That's why I turned it down. You had a weak moment and wanted to prove something."

"No, Jack, I didn't. And I'm glad you said no. Proves me right. You don't love me. You love Katie, I get that. But you won't ever truly love me."

"Believe what you want, Sara. Shannon has potential. I won't kid you. She's sharp, smart, an incredible salesperson, a hell of a lot like a particular woman I met at the door of an empty condo—after an about-to-be-married man had fucked her."

"You're an asshole."

"Yeah. Maybe. But one thing Shannon isn't—is you. You're just too damn stubborn to let me love you. So I'm moving on. Something I think I recall you telling me to do." He paused. Sara wanted to fill in the silence with something, anything.

"Listen, I gotta go. My family needs me."

"I'll tell Shannon you said hi."

"Don't be childish." His voice stayed low, making her scalp tingle. "I mean it. Don't assume you understand what my issues are. You'll never fully understand me."

"Okay Captain Obvious. Good luck. Jason and I will handle the hearing. Bye."

She hung up, tears running down her face. Jason stuck his head around the corner, sympathy in his eyes.

"Okay, I'll see you downtown at noon?"

She nodded, wiped her eyes, and turned on the computer. Jack's Skype account flared to life as the screen booted up. She frowned. They talked by phone or exchanged texts. Who would he be… she swallowed hard and clicked the conversation window labeled "Shannon."

"Don't read it. Don't read it. You are asking for trouble you don't want," the voice in her head chided her.

A fresh message dinged into his inbox. "Hey babe. Hope you're ok. Met Sara. She seems nice. Call me if you need to talk. I'm here, like we talked about. Let me be the emotional support you need."

The yell felt ripped from her soul. Her hand landed on the nearest thing, Jack's heavy business card holder, and she flung it across the room, hitting an expensive framed watercolor, sending them both crashing to the floor.

"Fucking asshole!" She jumped when Jack's secretary appeared, took one look at Sara's face, Jack's monitor, and the mess on the floor, and walked out. She sat, chest heaving, unable to focus.

Furious with him, but more with herself for being such a difficult bitch. Did she honestly think she deserved anything else at this stage of the game?

The Skype sound pierced her fog of misery.

Jack, with an answer. "Thanks. I still don't know where I'm at. I have enjoyed getting to know you—inside and out." The asinine little devil-horned emoticon made her ears buzz. A headache pounded her temples. She watched as they carried on a not-so-subtle sexy conversation, nausea rising at every exchange.

Dear God, what have I done? I pushed him away, straight into that woman's arms. Practically introduced them, helped unzip his… oh fuck.

She looked up when Jason snapped the computer screen off. He leaned on Jack's desk and studied her.

"He loves you."

"He's got a funny way of showing it."

"You won't meet him halfway, Sara."

"I did. And he rejected me."

"He told me about that." Sara rolled her eyes. Did she have no secrets? "You sort of blindsided him with it and he knee-jerk reacted. He wanted to take it back, trust me."

"Then why didn't he?"

"Because he's as bad as you are, dear." Jason patted her knee. "You two will either end up together or involved in some kind of mutual homicide. I have the office pool on it. Odds are on homicide, ever since..." He jerked his head to the hallway as Shannon breezed by. Sara flipped him off and stood.

"Can you find the damn files?"

"Sure thing."

• • • •

Chapter Twenty-One

Dear God, I hate soccer.

Sara sat, shivering under an umbrella on a late May afternoon as rain pelted down and her daughter and teammates sloshed through mud. "Playing under these conditions should be against some sort of safety law," she muttered under her breath.

"Oh Sara, don't be so negative." One of the soccer moms laughed. Sara frowned at her, but let her face soften into a smile. The woman had been the only team mom who had been nice to her. Not that she cared. She caught the eye of the coach, blushed, and looked away.

"Who's the new eye candy over there?" She leaned in to ask her new friend. "Did we get a new coach or something?" The guy was quite the vision, Tall, dark-skinned with long black hair tied back, his fit body hard to disguise under team colored shorts and a warm-up jacket.

It had been a long, lonely year since Jack returned from Germany, sister and family in tow. She was pissed-off at herself, but still stuck in her death spiral of "trust him/don't trust him."

Sara had paid her respects to Maureen as soon as Jack said she was ready for visitors. The poor woman had been vacant-eyed, lost looking and clung to her brother as if for dear life. Jack had found them a house, gotten the kids settled and in school, and, it seemed, deepened his dalliance with Shannon into a "relationship." He'd been brutally honest with her about that. Something she sometimes wished he wouldn't do.

But she'd asked for it, hadn't she?

Sara stayed aloof. She had to or risk losing her mind. She'd taken over a lot of the soccer duties against her will, but Katie loved it and she'd been determined to step up and be supportive. The yawning void labeled "Jack" ached like a sore tooth every day.

They'd passed so close, so many times, but always missed a real partnership, so she'd resigned herself to a life without him. Let Shannon have him. She'd already experienced his full self—they had met at that stupid club that he never took her to. Sara was certain they must share some kind of deeper connection.

Rat bastard.

She sighed and let herself admire the hot coach from a distance.

"He's the DOC," Lila said, breaking her reverie.

"Jargon alert. What the hell does that mean?"

"Director of Coaching. Kind of the boss of coaches. He's taking over our team."

"Oh." Sara bit her lip and crossed her legs. She'd gone out on a few dates, shared a few awkward, intimate moments with one or two of them, but she didn't have the energy for it. Not one, but two amazing men had entered her orbit, then left it, thanks to her own annoying obstinacy. She'd shut Jack and Craig out. And they got her message loud and clear. So she sat alone most nights, staring out the window, pondering her squandered opportunities.

The crowd murmured, the women primping as the sun broke through the grey overcast. Sara put her umbrella down and saw the reason for the commotion. Jack strode across the grass, impressive as always in his dark blue suit, expensive shoes and mega-watt smile. She observed him and the crowd's reaction and grumbled to herself. He shook hands, hugged women, and stood behind her, hands on her shoulders. His lips brushed her ear.

"How's she doing?"

"Fine." She moved her shoulders, so he'd get the hint. He did. Once the game finished, Katie ran over and jumped into his arms. Sara stood a little apart from the adoring Jack Gordon crowd. It startled her when a hand touched her arm.

"Oh, um sorry." She sidestepped the handsome man who stood too close all of a sudden. "Hi." She blushed and tucked a stray hair behind her ear.

"You are Katie's mom, no?" He closed the miniscule gap between them.

"Uh, yes. I am. And you are..."

He stuck his hand out. "Sorry. I'm Mateo. Mateo Alonso at your service."

She blushed again. He grinned, which sent a bolt of need to let his hair loose and run her fingers through it across her brain. She glanced over his shoulder and caught Jack's bright blue stare. She gave him a look she hoped relayed a "what?" message and refocused on the adorable, exotic young man.

Jack had no real reason to be unhappy. He had a job he loved, more than enough money in the bank, the respect of his peers, a beautiful girl he considered his daughter and as much time with her as he wanted. To top it off, there was a ready, willing, and able submissive in his life and his bed. She was full-on into the lifestyle, something he'd considered himself finished with. But he had to admit, he was enjoying their time together, if in a superficial way. It was as if he were play-acting with her, with pleasant results, mind you. Marking time with her as the Dom she seemed to need.

Because part of him would never give up on the possibility of being with Sara.

Ever.

When he got a load of the smarmy Italian stallion blatantly flirting with Sara not two yards away, his vision darkened and he had to clench the hand not holding onto Katie into a tight fist. It righted him, the pain in his hand. Reminded him he had zero say in Sara's life anymore.

They'd managed to misunderstand and mis-communicate themselves into some kind of bizarre, loveless, co-parenting arrangement that he, for one, despised even though, he reminded himself once more, he had no reason to be unhappy.

Right.

He ignored her all the way to the car, letting Kate's babbling recital of her two goals fill his head. A hand on his shoulder stopped the process across the grass. He arranged his face into neutral and turned, knowing who stood there as if she'd announced herself already.

Sara Jane Thornton—the woman who'd haunted his dreams his whole life for almost a decade. Beautiful, talented, sexy, killer manager, and the most frustrating female in the known universe, stood there, appraising him like he was a zoo exhibit. He returned her glare.

Kate tugged his sleeve. "Uncle Jack, can we do Washtenaw Dairy? Since we won? Like you said?" He smiled down at her. Evidence of the gorgeous woman she would someday be glowed from her like a beacon, with her deep green eyes and sharp, distinctive features, a brain and smart mouth to match. He grinned and crouched down to meet her gaze.

"A promise is a promise." He rose, trying to ignore the deep freeze coming from the woman who was the girl's mother. "You joining us, Sara?" He put a hand in his pocket, tried to calm the visceral fury at the sight of the soccer coach tool still watching her ass.

"Sure. Why not? Meet you there." She waved at the coach and smiled at him before climbing into her car without another word. Jack ground his teeth, shot what he hoped was a withering glare at the guy, who raised a hand before turning away.

By the time he pulled alongside the Ann Arbor institution that was Washtenaw Dairy, he'd calmed somewhat, forcing visions of Shannon through his brain, trying to remind himself he was in a place he liked with her.

It didn't work. He smacked the steering wheel, then jumped when Kate spoke.

"Uncle Jack? What's wrong?"

"Nothing, princess. Nothing at all. Let's go ruin our dinner together." He climbed out.

He ate his ice cream, not hearing anything anyone said, his entire focus on Sara, her lips, her hair—the little quirks he remembered, like biting her lip, rubbing the back of her neck. As nervous as he was, he supposed.

That was them, in a nutshell. Wanting one thing. Acting like they didn't. Screwing around—at least in his case—elsewhere to find relief. Why shouldn't she do the same?

He had to shut his eyes to hold down the tidal wave of fury at the thought of her with anyone else but him.

Jesus, Gordon. This is the twenty-first century. Stop thinking on a caveman level.

"Huh?" He looked down at Kate. Anger marred her face.

"Uncle Jack, aren't you listening?"

"No, sorry I wasn't." He grinned and pulled the girl onto his lap, loving her warmth and the unconditional love that poured off her in waves.

"I said I wanna spend the night at Ella's. She said Aunt Mo would take us ice skating later." Jack kissed her hair. Kate had grown close to his sister and her kids in the past year. He was surprised and pleased at how well they all fit together.

"Sure thing. Want me to drop you there now?"

She sighed and snuggled into his neck. He gripped her tighter, sudden emotion making his chest ache. Sara watched them, keeping silent.

"That's perfect. I have a date tonight anyway," he said, acting to type, fulfilling his role in this stupid charade, being the dickhead. He closed his eyes again, hating himself.

"Shannon again? She makes good pancakes. You guys save me some tomorrow, okay?" Katie said.

Sara rolled her eyes and sipped the last of her milkshake. Jack tried not to smirk. "No, Shannon and I are taking a break." He startled himself with this. But at that moment, it was exactly what he wanted to say, what he wanted Sara to hear. Sara narrowed her eyes at him.

"Okay. Good. You should take Mommy on a date. She never goes out." Kate jumped down and started kicking her soccer ball around the sidewalk. Jack stared at Sara, who avoided his eyes.

"That's sort of the idea." He kept his voice low.

She scoffed and tossed her cup into a nearby bin.

"No thanks, I um, already have a date tonight."

He raised an eyebrow, every inner alarm he had clanging around in his brain, bringing a headache that pounded his temples.

"Really?"

"Really. That such a surprise?"

"No." He leaned forward and grabbed her hand. The spark hit them both at the same moment. She caught her breath.

Mine.

Jack kept his gaze on hers. Her stare still had the power to rattle the shit out of him.

"Not a surprise. Cancel it. Go out with me."

She jerked her hand away.

"You don't have any say over me. Not anymore, remember?"

He leaned back. "

"I need to talk to you. No, scratch that. I want to buy you dinner, some place fancy, you pick. I'll even let you split the tab with me. Let's just talk." He hoped she didn't catch the desperation in his voice. Then again, maybe it would be better if she did.

He'd felt a lot of things about this woman in the course of his life with her. But today the compulsion tugged at his subconscious harder than ever, as if they'd never been apart, never fought, never said some of the shit they'd said to each other. She smiled, and he tried not to leap across the table and kiss her.

Jesus. Shannon—Remember Shannon?

He couldn't even picture her face at the moment. He made a mental note to fill her in on the whole "taking a break" thing later, to be fair.

"Fine. The Chop House. Eight o'clock. I'll be the one in the killer black dress." She stood. "Katie, c'mere and give me a hug."

The girl leapt into her mother's arms. Jack watched them together, his heart pounding in his ears.

Mine.

Sara berated herself all the way home. The hot soccer coach had flirted his ass off with her earlier. He'd even gotten her number. She'd kept the haze of ego-boosting buzz all the way to the ice cream place. Then, Jack had done it again.

She pounded the steering wheel.

"Shit! Shit! Shit!" Angry tears rolled down her cheeks. Was there ever a time the man didn't make her cry? She wiped her face, determined to make it the last time she let him do this to her.

Jack Gordon was not her future. They'd proven it time and again. Why he kept circling back, drawing her in, giving her hope.

But you let him, don't you? Is it because you need to prove he's yours, no matter who he's with?

No. It's because you love him. Just fucking well admit it.

She climbed out of her car and went inside, mentally playing the various conversations they might have after all these years that would mean anything.

On reflex she called her brother, needing his voice, his steady influence, even his outrage if she could get it.

"Hey," he answered, sounding breathless.

"Hey yourself. I didn't interrupt anything, did I? You sound busy."

He laughed.

"No. I just got back from a pick up soccer game." Sara smiled. Her new soccer mom friend Lila was considering something Sara had put in motion—to be Blake and Rob's surrogate.

"Oh. Well." She let the thought dangle.

"Don't worry. He's okay with it. A woman who loves soccer as much as he does? I think I'm the one who should worry this time."

"I'm going out with him tonight."

"Huh? Who?"

"Who do you think?"

"I thought he had... I mean, okay, good for you."

"I need you to go back to telling me to avoid him like the plague. Give me a reason to be logical about this."

"Too late for that. I think it's time to follow your heart."

"You are of no help to me right now."

"Tough. I'm gonna go. Lila's coming over for dinner."

"Be careful. She's coming off a nasty divorce. Asshole dumped her, made her move out and is trying to get full custody of..."

"We know."

"Well, um, I'm not sure what to say."

"You don't have to say anything. Nothing's happened. Yet."

"Right. Like I said, watch it. You boys might overwhelm her."

He laughed and must have handed the phone over to Rob.

"Sara. Go out with Jack, make up, marry him. Do something. Just quit dancing around it. We're all sick of you both."

"Stop bossing me, Freitag. And go easy with my friend."

"Ha. I can't keep her from undressing your brother with her eyes every time she sees him. Tell her to take it easy, why don't you?" But his voice stayed light and Sara had the thought that a full circle moment for those two might very well involve her fellow soccer mom. "Seriously, you and Jack need to quit the bullshit. Get it together. For Katie's sake? Hell, make her a little brother. I'm pretty sure you're capable of that."

"When monkeys fly. I will never be pregnant again if I have any say in it."

"Whatever. Go. Have fun. Love you."

On her way out the door, she got another call.

"Hey, handsome." She found lipstick, fumbled around for her car keys.

"Hi. How're things with you?" Craig's soft southern accent had deepened since his years spent in Nashville at med school. She loved the sound of it.

"Well, pretty good. I've got a date."

"Oh, sorry to bother you."

"No, no, I'm fine. Katie was asking about you today. You still taking her up to Traverse City for her tournament next weekend?"

"Yeah." He stayed quiet. Sara sat, sensing a problem.

"What's wrong? Spill it."

"Just wanted to hear your voice, I guess."

"Cut the crap. What's up?"

"Suzanne's being distant, like she's unhappy, but not really, but won't talk to me about it."

"She's been through a lot. Give her time. Be your amazing, charming self. She'll come around."

"You going out with Jack?"

"How in the hell does everybody know this already?"

"Because if you don't, the rest of us are gonna sue you for breach of contract or something."

"Jesus. That's pretty harsh, coming from you."

"Sara, you know how I feel about you. I just think it's time for you to own up to how you feel about him. Stop fighting it."

She stood, uneasy with the direction he was going. "You understand why I fight it. He's... impossible."

"Impossible to trust, you mean."

She sighed and ran her fingers through her hair. "Yes." But that old mental argument no longer held much air, even to her. He'd stuck around, been so amazing with Katie, and working with him as a manager of the brokerage had turned out to be a great experience on a lot of levels. The office considered them a work-married-couple and the pool on when they'd make it official had been ongoing for years.

"I should stop using that as an excuse."

"Sara, listen, you've heard it a million times, but I'm going to say it again, anyway. You guys are meant to be together. That doesn't mean it will be easy. But Jack loves you to distraction. Tell him what you want from him and he'll give it to you."

Face burning hot, she rose to her feet, sweaty and nervous like a teenager headed out on her first date. "See, that's the problem, right there." She sucked in a breath and gathered her thoughts. "I mean, I don't want something from him. I just want him. All of him, heart and soul. And I'm terrified that I won't get that. Ever. No matter what he says. I honestly think he's incapable of giving that to anyone."

"He'll do it for you. Trust me. But you have got to tell him—what you told me just now—about his heart and soul. Tell him that."

Pulse racing, she flopped onto her couch and stuck her fancy, high-heeled feet up on the coffee table. "It's like we're pre-programmed to fail. And I hate failure. So does he. But we keep doing it, somehow. We can't get this one thing right."

Craig heaved a long sigh. She smiled.

"I'm sorry. This isn't your problem and you have your own. I'm being selfish."

"One of your many charms," he said, chuckling into her ear.

"I'm feeling sorry for myself, I guess."

"Well stop it. Go out and get your man. Stop messing around."

"Yes sir. I'd say the same to you. Stop messing around and tell Suzanne you love and she needs to get over herself. Oh…" She stopped, hand to her lips, and closed her eyes.

"Yeah. Why don't you take your own advice, much?"

"How do you stand me? How have any of you stood either of us through all this time?"

"Because we love you, Sara. Why else? Me. Blake. Rob. Your parents. Julie. Even Suzanne. We're here for you, but we're also this close to shutting you guys in a room and locking the door behind you until you figure things out."

Sara burst out laughing. "That would never work. We don't do well with close proximity somehow, unless we're...." Her face flushed again.

"Here's the thing. I still have guilt about my part in keeping you guys apart at one time. But I did it because at the time, I did love you. But you were right about one thing. I considered myself in direct competition with Jack. Something few men would take on. I was in heady company, going out—okay, having a lot of sex—with you."

All her nerves went on high alert at these words. She launched herself up off the couch and headed for the bathroom to check her makeup. Not wanting to hear more from him, but knowing she had to.

"Blake feels bad about it, too. He realizes his part in the keep-Sara-from-Jack years was crucial. He thought he was doing you a favor, protecting you. I did too, on some level. But neither of us did either of you any favors."

"Wait, Craig... I...."

"No, I need to say this, and you need to listen." He blew out a breath. Sara closed her eyes, waiting for more. Even as her racing pulse calmed and her pounding heart quieted.

Because he was right. This was it. Tonight's date was her absolute last shot. On a long list of "last shots" they'd blown with their strong emotional barrier bullshit.

"You and Jack belong together, Sara. He's matured. So have you. You have a child together, for Christ's sake."

"Wait, that's..."

"No. Katie is his. We all know this without the benefit of a blood test. His whole thing with that agent in his office is nothing but a distraction, something to keep him from going nuts over the fact that you won't let him into your heart. Did you ever consider that?"

Tears welled in her eyes. She grabbed a tissue to blot them before they ruined her makeup.

"That's right, Sara. You can't expect him to hand over his, unless you're offering yours in exchange. That means you have to stop fronting, stop posturing, stop making excuses. You want him, right?"

She sucked in a breath, speechless at his outburst.

"Well?"

"Yes," she said, her voice barely above a whisper. "Yes. I do. I want him more than I want anything."

"Then tell him that. Stop making it so god damned complicated. Because it's not. I know he's never far out of your life. I'm willing to bet he's always giving you stuff, too. Am I right?"

She nodded, watching as the damn tears continued to fall, grateful for whomever invented waterproof mascara as she scrabbled around in her medicine cabinet for eye drops to hide the redness.

"Why are you saying all of this to me? Why now?" she asked after setting the phone on the vanity top and putting Craig on speaker.

"It had to come from me. I think you know why."

Blinking fast, she caught her gaze in the mirror again.

Jack.

You want him.

Offer your heart and soul.

Don't be afraid any more. Or you'll never be happy.

"Thank you," she said. "I don't know what else to say to you. This is so... weird."

He laughed, a sound that soothed her rattled nerves and made her smile. She put away the eye drops, applied lipstick and picked up her impractical, fancy, going-out bag. One Jack had given her at some point. She paused and looked around, noting all the things he'd gifted her with, including the necklace and earrings she was wearing right now.

Craig was right.

"I'm right, you know," he said, making her shiver at the way he'd mirrored her exact thought. "He shows his love by giving you stuff.

Working with you. Making Stewart Realty successful. By loving Katie so hard, you can read it on his face. It's time for you to own up to that. Let him love you his way, not some other way you've built up in your head is the only way."

"Damn, son, you sure you're not working in psychiatry instead of emergency medicine?"

He didn't laugh. "I loved you once, Sara, and it affected me in a way I can't explain. I want you to be happy and I get it now. That's only going to happen if you're with Jack."

"Okay," she said, pausing on her way to the door to look at herself in the full-length mirror. At that moment, her need to be in front of Jack, to take Craig's advice and tell him all the truths she'd held in her heart for so long about him, consequences be damned was so strong it was choking her.

She had to give him what he wanted—what he'd always wanted. To offer her trust, so he could offer his.

"Thanks again, Craig."

"You're welcome. Go get him, tiger."

She took a deep breath, clicked off the call, and headed out for her car.

Chapter Twenty-Two

Jack fiddled with his cocktail napkin, ignoring the blatant stare of the woman who'd chosen the empty bar stool next to him, despite the fact there were at least five other seats she could have taken. He did not need this, not tonight.

His mind spun, his entire body quivered like an exposed nerve ending. Gulping the bourbon, he signaled for another. When his phone buzzed with a text, he frowned, read it and typed out a reply: Sorry, needed a night off. Let's talk tomorrow.

Shannon shot back. Is it her? Just tell me now, Jack. I don't play games.

He set his jaw and answered her.

Yes. It always has been. I'm sorry. You're an incredible woman and I feel like shit for doing this, trust me.

She didn't answer, so he tucked the phone away.

What was his problem? Did he really need her in his life, no matter what his heart said? They weren't good together.

But yet, they were. Or they would be. If he'd open up, allow himself to be vulnerable.

Something he'd not done since... okay, you're a grown-ass man, Gordon. Time to stop using some chick dumping you in law school as an excuse to commit to Sara. You're asking her to do the same. You have to stop pretending, tear down your emotional blockades, be honest with her.

He shook his head at that mental gut check, turning to face the bar so the admittedly hot woman next to him wouldn't engage him, tempt him like he usually preferred. For a minor distraction, he snuck a look at her legs. She uncrossed and re-crossed them, obviously aware of his gaze. He laughed and looked up at her just as Sara entered the restaurant. He leapt up, not ready to get caught in some bullshit misunderstanding yet again.

He stopped, speechless. The black dress fit her like a second skin. Her figure had changed since pregnancy, but only for the better, as far as he was concerned. Her lightly tanned arms and shoulders sparkled. Diamond earrings and a drop necklace he'd given her last Christmas made him smile.

He loved buying her jewelry, mainly because it pissed her off, but she never turned it down, unless it came with a "Will you...," question attached. He caught himself more often than not buying her all kinds of stuff. None of which she ever refused. He loved doing things to make her happy, to help her be more successful, to bring her joy.

Okay, you lame ass, time to stop giving her stuff. Give her want she wants.

He sensed his barriers rising, excuses ringing in his ears—*she's prickly, temperamental, high maintenance, won't ever trust you. She makes you want to put your fist through the wall every other day. Why subject yourself to that? Right?*

Wrong.

He tucked his hands in his pockets and let her look around for a minute, so he could study her a bit longer. A lifelong cynic about love, Jack had no pre-conceived notions about the two of them. But he did know one thing, and seeing her flirt with that smarmy tool of a soccer coach had solidified it for him.

He stepped to the side into her line of sight. She smiled and his universe began to slide back into place.

Sara's breathing wouldn't settle. The whole car ride downtown, parking, the quick walk to the restaurant all kept that weird, first date vibe—ridiculous given their long history. But she decided to treat it like one. Squaring her shoulders before entering, she put on her best smile, forced herself to relax.

It's just Jack, for crying out loud.

She smiled at the deep meaning that statement had for her through the years.

A whoosh of cool air greeted her, a relief after the late spring heat outside. Suddenly nervous, she fiddled with her hair, bit her lip and looked around.

In a split second, the crowd parted like water, revealing him at the far end of the bar. He grinned, put his hands in his pockets, and she had to grab the back of a chair to remain standing up. She smiled, but her body ached with a sudden unmet need she hadn't even acknowledged. The invisible line connecting them took shape, shimmering, strong and inevitable.

Don't let him do this, Sara. You can resist it. You can...

But you don't want to, remember?

You want Jack. And not just his body, although that would be nice right about now.

"You are a vision of perfection." His voice rumbled through her like a thunderstorm on her horizon, ready to wreak havoc, and bring life-giving rain.

She stepped away, unable to stand his proximity that soon. He smiled and nodded at the host, who led them to the best table in Ann Arbor's best restaurant, tucked in the corner, near the front window. She sat, let the tuxedoed host put the napkin across her lap. He looked up at the waiter.

"Bourbon, double and a martini, up for..." he looked at her. "My date." She stuck her tongue out at him, but enjoyed the little a thrill at the way he handled it. She missed that, almost as much as the sensation of his lips and hands on her body.

The long years of motherhood, slogging through the days as a new manager, trying like hell to impress him, to prove he'd not taken a chance on her professionally without reason, had been exhausting. And lonely. But now, this whole scene, she had no idea where to put her hands, much less what to say to him.

Get a grip. You don't have to impress him. There's way too much water under your mutual bridge. Just be yourself.

"So, what's all this about, anyway?" She winced at how bitchy that sounded.

He touched the napkin to his lips, and she had to clutch her own soft linen cloth to keep from leaping across the table at him. Her hands shook, so she kept them under the table, leaving the martini untouched.

"A date, like I said." He sipped, never taking his eyes from hers. "No big deal." He held out a hand. She stared at it, then up at him. "I don't bite. I mean, unless you really want me to, that is." She frowned and then touched his palm, the ghost of an earlier Jack saying that very same thing to her flitting through her memory.

Regret, lust, and raw longing for everything about the man across from her nearly bowled her over. She took a bigger drink of the cocktail than she thought, and nearly choked. He laughed, stood and smacked her back, lingering over her bare skin much longer than necessary.

"You can switch off the full frontal seduction." Her voice sounded weak and breathy. She cleared her throat, tried to summon anger to cover whatever complicated craziness swirled in her brain.

He sat, stuck his feet out, seemingly relaxed, but she sensed something else. The loud restaurant quieted. All she saw or heard was Jack. His eyes, lips, familiar and comforting, irritating in a way, but needed. She gulped and hid her stress with the martini glass, remembering to swallow correctly this time.

"Sorry. Just being myself." He raised an eyebrow and his glass. She clinked hers against it. "So, what's your major?" She rolled her eyes.

"English. But I don't want to teach. I'll figure out something, I guess." She finished off her martini too quickly and stood. "I need to..." She turned and tried not to stumble away from the table.

Once she was in the luxurious ladies' room, she sat and put a wet paper towel over her eyes.

How in God's name could this end well? How did he manage to do this to her? Go out there and tell him what you want. Do what you came here to do, Sara.

By the time she made it back to the table, she was resolved. The fortress she'd constructed, torn down and rebuilt, usually in tears of anger over something stupid he'd done over the course of the last decade, was attempting to reform itself. She sensed it happening. It was up to her to put a stop to that.

You can't ask him to give you his heart and soul unless you're willing to do the same.

She smiled, tossed her hair back and made the crucial error of meeting his eyes. What she found there encompassed it all for her. The years, the heartache, the anger, the mistakes and the intensely physical attraction they'd had for each other. She sat in the chair he'd pulled out for her. His hand lingered on her thigh a tad longer than necessary for simple napkin replacement. She resisted the urge to swat his hand away, lest she drag him into the fancy bathroom and lock the door behind them.

She had to stifle a giggle at the memory of Craig's description of locking them in a room until they "worked things out."

"So, I'm thinking filet, but are you in a surf sorta mood? The lobster is on special." He studied his menu. She gaped at him, wondering why he didn't simply order for her. Whatever he chose would be perfect. She started to gnaw at her lip, then stopped when he grinned at her and reached across the small table to touch her cheek. "You choose."

"I, uh, whatever you think."

"All right then. But I'm getting a double order of those cheesy potatoes. Gotta keep you from licking the bowl and embarrassing me."

Sara laughed and her entire body relaxed in that instant. He ordered, after she picked the wine. They sat back, silent, appraising each other. She crossed her legs, letting one sexy shoe clad foot graze his calf. He raised an eyebrow. "You trying to seduce me, Thornton?"

"Hardly. It's kind of crowded at this really intimate table you chose."

His smile—the one she'd come to refer to as the Truly Happy Jack one—made her chest constrict and her face flush.

"Thanks for coming with me tonight. I've missed you."

"Well, you have a funny way of showing it." She smiled up at the sommelier as he presented, uncorked, and poured wine for her to taste. She nodded then looked back at the man who, had things gone as originally planned, would be her husband right now. "Sorry. That was catty. I'm the one who told you to find someone else and move on. I just... I mean, she's so pretty and young and. Oh never mind."

Jack swirled his wine, staring into the bowl as if it held all the answers.

"It's okay. I sort of sprung the Shannon thing on you. Frankly, it took me by surprise. We met at the club. And it, um, was..."

Sara held a hand up.

"Spare me."

He shook his head.

"I need you to hear this." He paused. Sara took the opportunity to study his face—the lines he'd developed around his eyes did nothing to diminish that rugged, not-quite-perfect-but-almost handsomeness she'd been so obsessed with at one time.

That you still are, Sara. After all these years. Which is why you're here, tonight, with him, remember?

"It's nothing special," he continued. "Like it always is there for me. Not much different from a solid workout. Then, um... afterwards, we talked. My manager's instinct kicked in and before I knew it, I had her, I mean. Oh hell, never mind." He sat back, his expression pensive.

Sara stared, shocked at how rattled he seemed. Not to mention how little his description of his club time with Shannon bothered her. Which told her a lot about how far she'd come. After a few moments, she leaned forward.

"Look, Jack, we have way too much behind us to…"

"Enjoy a nice, borderline romantic dinner?" He lifted his wine glass. "To… us. Whatever the hell that means." Sara laughed and touched her glass to his before taking a sip of the rich Italian red. She put her glass down, touched the soft napkin to her lips and decided to go with co-parenting chat to ease the tension.

"Katie says she has a boyfriend."

Sara had to jump up and smack his back to get him past his coughing fit. Leaning down, she put her lips to his ear, a little too close probably, but the need to get a familiar whiff of him overpowered her. "You okay?" She kept her hand on his shoulder, loving its strength under her palm.

"No. What the fuck?"

"Relax Uncle Jack. It's a crush."

"I won't have boys sniffing around…." Sara laughed so hard she got the hiccups. "It's not funny." He muttered into his glass.

"Oh yes, it is. You players are always the ones who end up with dau…" She stopped, took a sip of wine to cover her near slip.

"Yeah. I know." He left it at that.

As the meal progressed, they shared more laughter, memories, and light flirtation. Sara marveled at the man's ability to turn it on and off like a light switch. Serious about something real-estate-related one second, the next teasing her about the too-young-for-her soccer coach he'd watched her with that day.

She tried to avoid the one topic that burned her brain. Where, exactly, did they stand now? Why did he ask her out tonight? What was his arrangement, or situation, or relationship with Shannon, anyway?

"I needed her, for a time."

Sara blinked. Had she spoken out loud?

"Mainly because she needed me. The better, more mature and professional you get, the less you need me."

"You? Needy?" She scoffed. "Other than for pussy?"

He glared at her.

"I'll let that be the wine talking."

"Well, I'm glad that you got to be needed again." She let her voice rise at the end, more than a little incredulous. Jack ran his fingers through his hair, and Sara's entire body clenched with the desire to do the same exact thing—but plunge her fingers into hair when she kissed him and kissed him... and kissed him. She closed her eyes. The waiter cleared their dishes and started to present the dessert menu.

Sara looked up at him.

"We'll have the..."

"Crème Brule." Jack finished, his smile soft and one step shy of sappy. She looked down, realizing that if she went with what had flashed through her head, she'd be kissing him right now. "And two black coffees."

"And now?" She settled back in her chair. "Do you still need to be needed by Shannon?"

Don't ask a question you don't want the answer to Sara.

He shrugged. "I do know one thing." He leaned forward. She stayed still, resisting the compulsion to lean towards him, to meet him halfway.

"What's that?"

"You are amazing. No, seriously, you've turned that downtown office around, in spite of my meddling and budget cutting. You've headed off more crises than most managers combined. And you are a pure temptation on two legs in that dress."

"Oh, and you're gonna let me take credit, are you? No more I'm a 'Jack Gordon creation'?" She winced, but had to ask. It had rattled around in her head for years since he'd yelled it at her that last night at the party.

"I give you full credit for all of it. And shame on me for even thinking that, much less letting it pass my lips. I was an idiot. But I guess it's why you continually refuse to marry me."

She sat, unable to find words to express the roiling in her gut, the panicky fluttering in her chest.

Could it be? Jack had grown up?

Yes. He has. Now prove that you've done the same.

"And whoever picks out your jewelry is the bomb." She laughed, stuck her tongue out at him, and picked up her spoon to dip into the crisp caramelized sugar that coated her favorite dessert. A spoonful appeared from across the table at her lips before she could get her own bite. She opened her mouth and let the pure sin of eggs, cream and vanilla slide down her throat, shivering at the look in his eyes.

They finished in complete silence, comfortable, easy, and familiar. This time, when he held out a hand on the table, she took it, reveling in the now beloved snap and crackle of their connection.

"I'm not sleeping with you tonight. We clear on that?" she said, not meaning it. But meaning it at the same time. The last thing they needed was to fall into old habits—to fuck first, talk later.

Never mind, it was the only damn thing she wanted right now. Wanted it so badly she could feel his lips on her neck, his hands on her skin, his firm, familiar body next to hers.

"My dear, I wouldn't dream of it. Why spoil a perfectly good evening with a fight?" She laughed and pulled his hand to her lips, kissed it, then released him. "But," He would not let her break their eye contact. "I plan to kiss you, though. A lot. So be ready."

She blushed, got that first date thrill up and down her spine again, and picked up her coffee cup, never taking her gaze from his.

Jack sipped his coffee and watched her blush. No, they weren't going to end in the bed, or the floor, or the couch or the hallway or the car.

No, he admonished himself, again and with meaning. Tonight was about connecting on a different level. One they'd danced around so many times but never committed to.

His body did its usual horny thing, trying to convince him otherwise. He shifted in his seat and willed it down, willed himself to talk, to impress, to convince. And yet, at the same time, already breaking up with Shannon in his head. He realized he'd committed to at least one long-range date with her — a black-tie fundraiser he couldn't back out of gracefully. He'd just have to make her understand they went as friends, nothing more or less.

Sara.

She reached for the check when it arrived. He let her.

"Damn, Gordon, you're no cheap date." She tucked her credit card into the folder and smiled at him. Her green eyes lit up, and his heart soared. This was going to work. He'd be damned if he'd fuck it up again.

"A guy has to have his standards." He frowned when his phone buzzed, ignoring it. But when it stopped, then started again, he realized it must be an emergency.

"Jack," Maureen said. "I am so sorry to do this. You know I wouldn't normally but Katie hasn't been feeling well since she got here and now that she's still I took her temperature and it's right around a hundred. She wants to go home."

He sighed and looked at his date.

"Well, your daughter is sick. We have to go pick her up."

"What?"

"Yeah." He watched her sign off on the tab and tuck her card away.

"How is Maureen doing, anyway?" He slipped an arm around her waist as they walked toward the door.

"As well as can be expected, I guess. She was an absolute mess for a while. Brandis lived, you know, after the asshole drunk driver essentially pinned him against a tree. He held on so he could tell her he loved her one more time." Jack stopped outside the restaurant, looked up at the sky. A light breeze ruffled Sara's hair, and he couldn't resist the urge to reach out and tuck it behind her ear. "I loved that guy like a brother, you know?" Alarmed at the emotion rising in his chest, he cleared his throat and tucked her hand into his arm.

"I'm sorry." She leaned into him. "That's horrible."

"I'll meet you at her house, okay? I know it's my night but Mo said she thought Kate might want her Mama, being sick and all."

Katie lay tucked up on the large couch, bracketed by two enormous German shepherds who looked like they were guarding her. Jack grinned and sat beside her, putting a hand to her forehead.

"You're like an oven, Miss Kate. No wonder Hans and Fritz want to snuggle." She gave him a weak smile and climbed into his arms. He carried her into the kitchen, where Mo and Sara were talking.

"Sure you guys don't want a glass of wine or something?" Mo's eyes were still so haunted, her skin pale and fragile-looking. He'd never stop worrying about her. Sara gave her a big hug. She looked surprised at first, then happy. "Sorry." She let go, wiped her eyes. "I'm a leaking sieve."

Sara nodded, looking close to tears herself. Jack shifted Katie in his arms.

"I think we should get her to her own bed." He shot Sara a look, realizing their ability to communicate without words. If she gave him a high sign that Mo needed them to stay, he'd put Katie back on the couch and stay. The slight shake of her head gave him his answer.

"Yeah, probably." She turned back to Mo. "You have my number. Call me anytime. Ella and Adam are always welcome to come over if you need some.... well, anyway." Mo nodded, gave her brother a hug, and walked them to the door.

"She's such a doll." His sister touched Katie's bare leg. "A tomboy one minute, a bossy princess the next. And that temper... well, let's say I've seen that before." She pressed her lips to Jack's cheek and opened the door.

• • • •

"OKAY, I GAVE HER SOME of that liquid ibuprofen, got her a bath, and now she only needs goodnight kisses."

Jack rolled his sleeves back down as he walked into Sara's living room, determined to leave, to not drag this out any further, no matter how much he wanted to. Sara handed him a glass of wine and headed upstairs. He followed her legs with his gaze. They were bare, well-remembered, and delectable as she made her way up.

They sat on her couch later, his arm around her, their legs stretched out on the ottoman in front of them. "Should I worry about her? I mean, she's says she's sore all over and stuff. Just the flu?"

"You have your own in-house medical counsel on that, I think. Call one of them." She sighed and leaned into him, making his heart beat faster.

"Maybe later. This is nice."

He put their glasses on the side table and tilted her chin up. "I'm pretty sure I put kissing on the agenda." He slanted his mouth over hers, tasting her, reveling in the familiar sensation of her lips. He got serious with it, sweeping into her mouth with his tongue, sliding his fingers into her hair with one hand.

His body was sending signals he wouldn't acknowledge, so he broke away. She started to climb up into his lap, but he stopped her, stood, and got a grip on his purpose.

"I'm gonna go. Let's let this one sit, shall we? I don't have the energy or inclination to argue with you tonight."

She stared at him. "But we don't always argue after..."

"Yeah, actually, we do. I want to develop a new pattern. So I will kiss you goodnight, like a gentleman, and be on my way." He held out a hand, fighting everything in him that screamed at him to claim her now, take her. She wanted it. He knew it as surely as he knew his own shoe size. She sat, not moving. "C'mon baby. Give a guy a break. I'm trying..."

She took his hand, rose, and eased into his arms like she'd never left. Her own kiss spoke volumes. The sensation of her breasts, mashed to his chest, of her cool hands on his face forced him to use all the willpower he could muster not to toss her down on the carpet and make that connection he'd been missing for so long. Something he'd tried to recreate with Shannon but had failed to do. When she broke away, tears glistened in her eyes.

"No crying Sara. Not tonight." He stepped back, found his jacket, and headed for the door.

"Jack, wait."

He stopped without turning.

"I, I want you to stay." He shrugged into the suit coat and slowly faced her.

"I want to stay too. Which is why I'm leaving. Let's sleep on it and talk again tomorrow." Before she could say anything else, he blew her a kiss and walked out the door, cursing at and congratulating himself at the same time.

Chapter Twenty-Three

"Sara, I am so sorry!"

Craig looked frazzled, so she tried not to sound too pissed.

"I've still got no seniority in the group. When one of the other docs has to take time off, I have to pick up the shift." He flopped into the chair opposite her desk. She mentally ran through the options for the weekend. She had planned to get caught up on some paperwork on Saturday in the quiet, but it was nothing that couldn't wait.

An email from Mateo appeared on her monitor. "I'm so sorry you are not coming up to Traverse City with us. I would have liked to buy you a drink." She blushed and deleted it. That guy had no business being interested in her, much less flirting so relentlessly. It was a buzz, of course. Any woman her age would be flattered.

But she had a different goal in mind. One that didn't involve panty melting soccer coaches.

She reached for her phone and dashed a text to Jack, cancelling their date. Disappointment pierced her brain. She'd planned a serious seduction scene for that night at her place.

He'd been true to his word all week, sending her funny texts, an obnoxious display of roses, even a bottle of her favorite expensive champagne with a note that set her libido disco dancing:

"I remember sharing a bottle of Dom just like this one with you one night. I'll never forget how I licked it off your neck when you drank from the bottle. Then off your shoulder, your arm, your breasts. Here's to more of that, soon. But not too soon.

Love, Jack"

It all ramped her up so high she'd started keeping her vibrator under the pillow for emergencies. Everyone at her office was to watching the scene unfold with bated breath, something she didn't care for as it distracted them from their jobs. But there was nothing she could do about gossip.

She was ready for this. And she was determined to stuff her old, untrusting self into a garbage bag and toss it out. Anything if she could finally be with Jack for good.

She put a hand on Craig's shoulder to make him stay as she stepped out to have a quick conversation with her secretary, then shut the door. Sitting in the chair next to him, she stared hard into his brown eyes. "So?"

He ran a hand over his light red beard. "We're taking it slow, like she wants. She's so guarded. So enthusiastic about, um, sex." He blushed. "But when it comes to anything beyond physical, she shuts it off like a light bulb. Reminds me of some other frustrating female."

He stood, pulled her to her feet and into his arms. She sighed, breathing him in, remembering.

"But I'm gonna stick it out with her. My odds are better this time, I think." He kissed her lightly on the cheek. "Sounds like you're taking my advice about Mr. Gordon."

She leaned back. "How would you know that?"

"Small town, small world." He nodded at the enormous vase full of roses behind her on the credenza. "That's a seduction bouquet if I ever saw one."

She smacked his arm. He put his palm against her cheek. She closed her eyes and let herself lean into it, loving the warmth of it, of their onetime connection that had morphed into friendship. "I'm sorry about the weekend. Don't chicken out," he said. "I mean it."

"I won't," she assured him. "And don't worry. Weekend is covered."

Katie did nothing but whine all the way home from school when Sara broke the news that Uncle Craig had to work. Sara fed her a snack and tossed her in the bathtub with little conversation, biting down on the urge to scream at her to stop sniveling. To tell her life was full of disappointments and that she'd gotten her own way too often. The girl hadn't felt a hundred percent for several days, although the pediatrician claimed there was nothing wrong with her now that the fever had passed.

Hey sexy. She smiled at Jack's regular evening missive.

Hey yourself. Busy. Packing.

Right. So do you want me to come too? I was gonna take Mo and her kids up north, anyway.

No, she's expecting you to watch them so she can go to the spa on Sunday. She told me. Do NOT stand her up. She needs it. We can always reschedule our date.

All right. Have Kate call me after her games.

Will do.

She set the phone on the bed, threw the necessary items in a bag, locating all of Katie's soccer paraphernalia. After a long hot shower, she plucked the girl from the couch and deposited her into the car, along with her tablet for movies and a pile of coloring books and her marker collection. Katie sniffled, then snuggled down on her pillow. Sara sighed. She wasn't looking forward to the three and a half hour drive up to the Grand Traverse Resort after not sleeping well all week herself. She drove through a coffee shop for a double espresso before getting onto the interstate. It wasn't until she'd stopped to pee that she noticed her phone had five unread texts.

One from her brother.

I'm bringing Maddie up. I hear you'll be there. Wanna carpool?

She read the next few texts, two from Lila letting her know that the date with Blake and Rob had indeed gone very well and that Blake was bringing her daughter, Katie's teammate and friend Maddie to the tournament so she and Rob could have some time alone.

Sara smiled into the darkened car.

Small fucking world.

Then she read one from Mateo that made her ears burn.

I hear you are coming. Can you meet me tonight? I'll be in the rooftop bar.

And then Jack, one she must have missed at the end of their conversation.

I love you. Don't tell anybody. I have my reputation.

She tossed the phone into the passenger seat, cranked her tunes, and sped through the rapidly darkening night.

Jack kept checking his phone, trying not to be pissed that she never responded to his last text, wishing he'd hadn't sent it, and attempting to concentrate on the crisis du jour. Shannon walked by, shooting him an inscrutable look before he indicated the phone conversation he was having took priority over her pique. The breaking it off thing had not gone as smoothly as he would have hoped. The woman had said some spot-on things about him, and about him and Sara. But he'd heard it all before. It no longer had any power to hurt.

He shut the door, and finished arguing with a fellow broker manager about a stolen listing, then hung up, digging his knuckles into his eyes. God, he'd give anything to be driving them up to that tournament right now. He had a standing upgrade at that resort and could get them a condo.

But he'd promised Mo he'd help her out this weekend. He grabbed his phone and keys and headed for the door as his phone rang again.

"Hey babe. What's up?"

Mo sounded chipper for a change, more like her old self.

"I rescheduled my spa weekend. Gonna take the kids out to Brandis's parents' place on Zukey Lake instead. You're invited, if you want to come up."

"Why? Didn't you want the pampering thing? Kids and I had our weekend planned down to the pancakes and ice cream for breakfast."

"No. I'm good. Another time."

"Well, alright, but if you change your mind..."

"I won't. Why don't you go up to Katie's tournament?"

She hung up. Jack grinned, no longer quite so exhausted as he raced home to pack.

He rolled into the resort around ten p.m. The lobby teemed with squealing soccer players and their getting-drunk parents. He got his condo upgrade, stashed his suitcase, then headed up to the rooftop bar. He caught sight of Blake sitting with a couple of the dads.

He shook Sara's brother's hand. "What are we drinking?"

After about thirty minutes of chitchat and beer, he surmised that Lila had auditioned for the role of surrogate mom and had passed with flying colors. Jack smirked. He figured it wouldn't be long before Freitag worked a female into their mix. Blake certainly wouldn't complain.

"Hey, where's Sara?"

Blake shrugged. "Getting a massage, I think." He finished his beer and glanced at his phone. "Girls are back from the pool," he said. "I'm feeding Maddie and Katie in our room. Sara has pool and dinner duty tomorrow night." He shook hands with Jack and made his farewells to the other parents. "Want me to tell Katie you're here?"

"I told her I was coming, that it was a surprise for Sara."

"Ah, okay then." Blake paused. "You guys are…"

"Working it out, I think. I hope." He held up his glass. "With your blessings?"

Blake smiled and slapped his shoulder. "It's been a long time coming. But would you mind picking up the pace a little? My money's on a beach wedding inside of six months and I hate to lose a bet."

Jack ordered another beer and talked soccer, real estate, and other generalities with the growing group of parents around the bar. One dad bought a round of Irish whiskey. Jack reciprocated. The crowd got bigger and louder.

He found himself with a fresh beer in front of him and sitting next to one of the moms. Confused, on a direct path and do-not-pass-go to shitfaced, he looked down and saw the mom's hand on his thigh. Way high up, in fact. He shook his head to clear it, then turned to see whose hand it was.

Sara. Where the hell was she? He'd never known her to pass on an impromptu event like this.

The woman, he thought her name was Denise, or maybe Danielle, was way too close for comfort. Her hand slid even further up his leg, came into direct contact with his crotch. He flinched. He'd had too much to drink. The bar noises seemed to ramp up, filling his ears with laughter, too-loud conversations, the occasional drunken, female screech.

"Okay, all right, easy does it," he said, chuckling and attempting to extract himself from the woman's clutches. She was one of those way-too-thin types, with a boob job, if he wasn't mistaken and he rarely was. The horny vibes rolled off her in waves. He pried her hand off his zipper, put it back in her lap, patted it, and smiled. "Flattered, but no thanks."

She pouted, her collagen-injected lips mesmerizing him in a way that reminded him he had consumed way too much brown liquor for his own good. "Can I buy you a drink?" were the words on his lips, ever eager not to insult anyone for an honest attempt at drunken, on-the-road seduction. He smiled at the woman's fake tits and was raising his hand to get the bartender's attention when he realized she was all up in his personal space bubble. She had her hand planted back on his thigh, and her lips were on his.

He tasted the booze first, with a back-whiff of something sickly sweet, and cigarettes. Before he his alcohol-soaked nerves reacted, the damn woman had her tongue in his mouth. He put his hands on her shoulders and gave a firm push, disconnecting their lips with a sound that made him nauseated.

"Come on, Jack," she said, her voice loud to be heard over the obnoxious ruckus of the bar. "You've been staring at me all night." She shifted, arching her back to ensure he didn't miss the significance of her cleavage. "No one's watching. Why don't you let me..." She licked her lips at the same minute she touched his trouser-covered dick, which remained at parade rest, something he'd thank the booze for, not to mention he was no more turned on by this predatory female than he would be a car full of scary clowns.

"Like I said," he insisted, plucking her hand off him once again, trying not to raise his voice. "Flattered. But no." He glanced around, motioned for the bartender and asked for a glass of water. The guy brought it and he downed half in a few long gulps, only half aware that Denise/Danielle was still sitting too close to him.

He finished the water, signaled for more, knowing at this stage it was only a way to fend off a hangover. "Have you seen Sara?" he asked the walking boob job next to him.

She turned away and faced the bar, her thigh still touching his, her red-nailed hand wrapped around a disgusting-looking green drink in a martini glass which would account for the sickly sweet taste on her lips earlier. "I haven't. Maybe check in the coach's room?" She glanced over her shoulder at him, her face a mask of disgust, or maybe frustration.

Jack shook off the need to ask her if she was okay, even as his brain processed what she'd said. "Um, what?"

The woman waved a dismissive hand in his face and drained her drink. He blinked, trying to sort out what was going on. Jesus, he'd only had two shots of whiskey and three low-octane beers. He'd turned himself into a lightweight. His head dropped as he focused down on the bar's top.

"Don't be sad, Jack. You're way too hot to be sitting here all alone." Denise/Danielle wouldn't give up on him. At one point, he realized one arm was around his shoulder, one rock-hard tit pressed against him, her ever-eager other hand crawling up the inside of his thigh yet again. When he felt her tongue in his ear, he stood up, knocking over his half-empty second glass of water.

"Back off, okay," he said, holding up a hand and looking around to make sure the now teeming crowd hadn't noticed.

Sara. He needed to find Sara.

"Check in the coach's room."

After wiping off his face, and accepting that his general exhaustion level wasn't mixing with the liquor sloshing around in his system, he realized that detaching from his eager bar buddy was going to be harder than usual. Woman was persistent, he'd give her credit for that. She was at his side, having made her way over to him in an eye-blink, one arm around his waist, the other resting on his chest, her lips to his ear. "Let's go, hot stuff. I've been waiting to get you alone for a while."

I am living out some bizarre hellscape. Something that's proving a point to me, he thought, as he pulled her off him with a near-audible sucking noise.

"Check the coach's room."

As he thought that he fucking well would go do that, if this crazy woman would get her tentacles off him, the elevator door out onto the rooftop bar slid open, and more people spilled out of it. Then he saw her. Sara, leaning against the back of the elevator. Relieved beyond measure, he glanced over at the woman he'd swear had been put in his path so he could prove something, but was taking her karmic responsibility to tempt him way too seriously. Her lips were parted in something resembling a smile. She puffed herself up, sticking those synthetic tits even higher into the air and drawing a fair few male eyeballs around them. Her lollipop of a head—too big for her frame, given its emaciated state—tilted, drawing his gaze to the back of the elevator.

He took a step forward without thinking, only wanting to drag Sara off the elevator and shove her at Denise/Danielle. To show her, "this is why I'm not interested in you, so back the hell off." Sara seemed anxious and nervous, something he sensed, as if he were experiencing it himself. Worried, he took another step forward when the rest of the elevator emptied, leaving Sara. And Matteo, his daughter's soccer coach, standing too close together.

He saw it all in a split second—too fast, considering the past fifteen minutes of his own life. What he didn't see—the unhappiness on her face, the tension in her stance, her eyes moving around, seeking escape. What he saw—the proximity of their bodies, the dark-haired, much younger man's fit physique in black jeans and a form-fitting white shirt, and the way he pressed his face into Sara's neck, or her ear.

He heard a loud roar from somewhere and took the fifty feet to the elevator and stepped inside, right in front of her. His ears were full of a scary whooshing noise, blocking the bar's cacophony as she disentangled from the smarmy asshole's arm. He stood like some kind of macho shithead, his stance a clear message of "back off, this one's mine."

Mine.

Jack shut his eyes and attempted to wrestle his inner mature, twenty-first century, enlightened, the-future-is-female, I've-sworn-off-strip-bars, male to the surface. This was not what he thought it was. Shit, if she'd shown up five minutes ago, she would've caught him in a clinch not of his choosing. This was, to be sure, some kind of test. Something to make him prove to himself and to her that he was better than his sexist, double-standard, mostly misogynist upbringing.

"Jack...," a voice intoned from somewhere behind him.

His eyes flew open. He stared at Sara as she stared at someone behind him, even as he felt a hand on his arm, tugging him out of the elevator, pulling him to her like a super magnet. The doors began to close. His arm shot out, blocking them.

Sara's eyes narrowed. She shook off the coach, and stood in front of him, arms crossed, green eyes blazing in a way he recognized from all the times he'd seen her furious for one reason or another. The sum total of their relationship was here, right now, with some woman's possessive hand on his arm and some guy's looming, young-man-sexy presence looming next to her.

"What are you doing here? I told you Mo needed..."

"Mo cancelled. Thought I'd surprise you."

The surreal nature of this conversation wasn't lost on him. He stuck his hands in his pockets, without shaking off Denise/Danielle's fingers, which were digging into his biceps.

The testosterone level in the small space ramped up, wavering and visible to his eyes. A bolt of raw jealous fury tore through him. Dear God, he was a fool to think this would ever work. The universe seemed designed against it, if this stupid scene was any sign. The reality of his gut-deep fury at the sight of her, in a weird moment with that damn kid, proved one thing to him.

She wasn't the only one who didn't want to get hurt. She wasn't the only person who couldn't trust. And this proved to him what his problem was. He wanted nothing more than to make her admit she wanted him back, that she loved him, that she'd been wrong all these years. But once that happened, what in the hell would he do? Did he even have what it took to sustain a relationship beyond that?

The memories of the deep hole of misery he'd had to clamber out of all those years ago smacked him upside the head, making his face burn hot and his hands curl into fists. It was happening again. His emotional barriers were clashing together, clanging shut. Head suddenly clear, he took a step away from the open elevator doors. "I'll leave you to your... chat."

The bar darkened around him. A primal, un-woke, get-your-hands-off-my-woman caveman retro asshole in him roared in his ears, urging him to act. The simple act of moving to the left and pressing the other elevator's down button took more effort that he thought he could manage.

"That's more like it, baby," his new friend purred in his ear. He glanced down, shocked to find her still there. "My room's on the ninth floor." Without a word, he pushed the number nine, rode down to the ninth floor with her, his mind in a kind of white-noise, non-space.

When the doors opened, he pulled her arm off him and gave her a gentle push out into the hallway.

"But..." she protested, turning and giving him another arched back, don't-miss-my-boobs posture.

"Bye," he said, pressing the close door button before slumping back against the wall without pushing any more buttons. When he realized the thing was headed back up, he groaned, wanting nothing more than fresh air, a shower, or to put his fist through a wall. The doors opened. Sara was standing there, of course, arms crossed, no hot-stuff coach in sight.

"God dammit Jack, you don't know what..." He took a breath and looked at her. Everything about her screamed sexy. And that pipsqueak asshole of a washed up athlete had tried to move in on her.

"I can't talk to you right now. I need air." He hit the close door and then ground buttons, and took a last look at her before the doors slid shut. Slumping against the railing, he tried to calm his clamoring brain and shaking body. He didn't know what to say to her, anyway. What he'd seen wasn't what he thought it was. He also knew that his visceral reaction to it was not a great indicator of how well he could handle giving her what she wanted from him—his unwavering love, trust, and his beating heart.

He strode into the downstairs, much more low-key bar, offered the guy a hundred-dollar bill for a bottle of Jefferson Reserve, and without a glance at anyone, walked out and towards his condo.

Shock and adrenaline kept Sara's tears at bay when she slammed her finger into the down button, furious at him for assuming anything about her. She'd not even planned to go up to the bar, but Denise, one of the moms on the team, had told her she was missing out on a fun party. That she needed to get her butt upstairs in the next few minutes or she'd miss out. It was kind of strange, since Sara didn't consider herself close to any parents on the team other than Lila. Befriending everyone was Jack's area, not hers.

Katie was in Maddie's room eating dinner with Blake. She'd tried to relax, to read a book, not to obsess over missing out on her seduction night. But when the text from the woman had hit her screen, she'd tried to place her, then recalled she was one of the single moms on the prowl types who'd shown up one game with a fresh set of tits.

Well, why not have a drink if it would help dispel her regret at being here and not in the smack middle of making love with Jack? She'd even bought a set of simple rings, platinum bands that cost almost as much as a decent diamond engagement ring she'd planned on presenting to him. She was going to ask him to marry her, and she knew he'd say yes.

Ah, best laid plans, she thought as she refreshed her makeup and pulled her hair back in a ponytail. A nice glass of wine and some team parent gossip might be exactly what she needed right now.

Matteo had been walking toward the elevator, and she wanted to bolt. She'd backed around the corner and taken a deep breath. She didn't want any part of this guy. And had no intention of riding an elevator with him.

"Sara?"

She flinched, cursed under her breath, and rounded the corner. "Hi, Matteo."

He smiled. Dear Lord, he was a specimen. But that's it. Eye candy. She decided to relax and go with it. Riding a damn elevator wasn't going to hurt anything. "Hi. Can I buy you a drink?"

"Sure," he said, holding out his arm. They stood with a respectable three feet between them. Then, the damn thing stopped at every floor up, filling with more parents seeking booze. By the time it reached the rooftop bar, she'd had to tell Denise twice she was "on her way" via text twice. She and Matteo were crushed back against the wall and pressed together by sheer necessity given the crowd.

She didn't realize his arm was around her until the doors opened, bringing fresh air and relief. As the thing emptied, she looked around, seeking the woman who'd summoned her, wanting to escape from the uncomfortable closeness of the man next to her. It seemed to take forever to get everyone out. She tried to move away from him, but his arm tightened around her.

She spotted Jack, which confused her for a split second. The next second, she felt Matteo's lips near her ear, his breath hot on her neck. She blinked fast, noting how he looked at her, then at the man glommed onto her.

No. Not now. Not this.

His eyes narrowed as he rushed forward and stood in front of her. She shook the other man off her and watched as he stood, legs spread, arms crossed, face a mask of "back off, I'm with her."

Tears burned, but she held them back. She could explain. It would be fine. This was ridiculous. But the look on Jack's face made her heart sink down somewhere around her feet. Then she caught sight of Denise, the woman who'd told her to "get up here and party."

Fury roared in her ears when the woman spoke Jack's name in a way she recognized from all the time she'd spent coping with the realities of Heather, and then Shannon. Jack seemed to shut down, his expression closing up as he took a step back toward the woman who was pulling him away. As she watched, her feet seemed to be stuck in glue. The doors started to slide shut. Jack's arm stopped them.

"What are you doing here? I told you Mo needed..." she began, her voice shaky.

"Mo cancelled. Thought I'd surprise you."

As she watched, Jack's face seemed to go through a myriad of emotions, settling on disdain, or perhaps nonchalance. She wasn't sure what was worse. She opened her mouth to say something to dispel the stupidity of this scene.

"I'll leave you to your... chat," Jack said, pre-empting her. She watched him with Denise still attached to him move to the left and stroll into the other elevator. She ran out, tried to stop him, but the doors closed between them. The numbers counted down to nine, then back up. She knew, like she knew the color of her own eyes, that he hadn't gone to Denise's room with her. And sure enough, the doors opened, revealing him again in all his dark-blue-trousered, dress-shirted glory. She bit her lip. God, but he was so perfect. Even his dark, angry glare made her weak in the knees.

"Goddamnit Jack, you don't know what...," she began, confident she could convince him it was a silly misunderstanding. Proud that she wasn't even jealous of the way Denise had acted and of her confidence in him—her trust—that he'd be back.

"I can't talk to you right now. I need air," he said before the doors closed between them again, leaving her standing alone, her heart racing, wondering if there would ever be a time she could get this right.

She sensed Matteo before she saw him. She turned to him. "I'm sorry. I didn't mean to give you the wrong idea."

He smiled and touched her cheek. "No, I'm sorry. I didn't realize you and Katie's father..."

"No, no, he's not, I mean. Oh hell." The tears let loose then, rolling down her face, blurring her vision. She slumped against the wall between the elevators. "I have to go find him." He nodded and pressed the down button for her.

She rode the thing to the ground floor, mind blank, ears ringing, heart thudding and making her breathless. How could she fix this? Jack was so stubborn, so unwilling to listen to her.

So much like you, Sara.

She stopped on her floor and knocked on Blake's door. "Sara? You okay?" She saw Maddie and Katie, both curled in a chair with a book.

"Yes. No." She collapsed into a chair. "Jack's here."

"I know." He handed her a water bottle. "What happened?"

"Nothing. Everything. The usual I guess." She sighed and reached for his hand. "I need to go find him."

"Okay."

Katie rubbed her eyes and looked up at Sara. She knelt down at her daughter's eye level. "Honey, I'm gonna go see Uncle Jack, okay? Can you sleep here in Uncle Blake's room with Maddie?" The girl nodded and yawned.

"He texted me. Told me not to tell you he was on his way. He wanted to surprise you. Were you surprised, Mommy?" Sara tried not to cry and scare the girl.

"Yeah, he did. Be sure to brush your teeth. I'll take you both to breakfast in the

Chapter Twenty-Four

After pleading with the front desk to give her Jack's condo number, she started down the darkened path, lighting the way with her phone. She stumbled once, not paying attention to the landscaping. Music poured from the open, well-lit windows. It took four tries knocking, plus her yelling at him to get any response. He threw the door open and leaned on the doorway, half empty bottle of bourbon in hand. She grabbed it and took a big gulp, letting the fiery alcohol scorch its way down her throat.

He shrugged and headed back inside. He'd stripped to his dress trousers, and the firm line of his bare shoulders made her shiver. If things had worked like they should have, she'd be seducing him right now, on her big white rug in her living room, followed by a sincere proposal. Not standing here like an idiot trying to explain a scene she had no explanation for. One she shouldn't have to explain since nothing had happened.

And stuck in a mud pit of remorse for realizing that this is what she'd done to him so many times. It was a miracle he even spoke to her, much less wanted to rekindle things.

Squaring her shoulders, she marched in behind him. After finding the Bluetooth speaker and turning down the pounding music, she had to go out the sliding glass door to find him. He'd parked himself on the patio, bare feet up on a table, staring out onto the darkened golf course. She slid into the seat next to him.

"I see why you were so adamant that I stay behind."

"No, you don't."

"Actually, I do. Don't kid a kidder. I know a diversion when I see it. Hell, I've used them myself."

She swallowed the retort. Getting mad would come across as defensive. And she knew, deep in her gut, that he was fronting. She had to go carefully, plus she had no reason to be defensive. She had done nothing wrong. They'd both been caught in bizarre circumstances, as if on purpose, to put them through this particular pace to prove something.

"Why are you here?" he asked.

"Because I... I wanted to make sure you were okay." She clutched her shaking hands together in her lap, willing better words from her throat but unable to conjure them.

"I'm fine. Now leave. I think I can say with full authority that we are through. I can't take this anymore."

"You? You can't take it? How do you think I felt when I got to meet your surprise new toy slash girlfriend while I was trying to manage your office for you?" She heard her voice rise and hated herself for bringing it up. That would only raise the ante. Which it did.

"I explained it to you. And told you we'd broken it off. So I could work this shit out with you. Jesus." He grabbed the bottle and knocked back another long drink. "But I didn't realize the full-on cougar you'd turned into. Nice one. He's young enough to go all night. Unlike some of us old guys."

She stood. "I trust you Jack. Even in the face of my fellow soccer mom, clinging to you like a limpet. But you see one thing and misinterpret it and I'm the reason we're 'through?'" She moved, so she was standing in front of him, looming over him as he lounged, loose-limbed and definitely drunk. "I can see that I'm not the only one with trust issues here. You'll never grow up and get past her, past what's-her-name—Jenna. Jesus, man, it's been how many years?"

He rose, forcing her to take a step back. Without a word, he picked her up and carried her inside. Shocked, angry, but her body already responding to him, she shrieked when he tossed her onto the massive bed.

"I should have done this the other night. I shouldn't have waited." He tugged her shirt up and off. Unclasped her bra and had it on the floor in seconds. "I fucking love you. How many times, how many ways, do I have to prove it?"

She sucked in a breath at the sight of tears standing in his bright blue eyes. He narrowed them and then all she knew was his mouth, lips and tongue. She groaned and wrapped herself around him, but he shoved her down, pinned her wrists with one hand, tugging her jeans and panties off with the other.

"Mine." He muttered into her neck. The licks and nibbles took on a painful edge, making her sigh and her body pulse in immediate response. "Fucking mine."

"Oh God, yes!" she yelped, clutching his hair, his shoulders, anything and anywhere just to touch him. He teased her outside and in, then stopped as she was about to climax. He stared at her, brought his fingers to her lips, then to his, leaving her writhing with need.

He focused on her nipples next, sucked and tugged on them so hard it brought tears to her eyes. He worked his way down, sucking and biting her flesh, until he reached her center. Their ragged breathing echoed in the room. "Please, Jack," she whimpered. "I need..."

He lowered his mouth to her clit, fucking her with his fingers and tongue so hard she had to bite her own hand to keep from screaming with ecstasy. But he kept on the edge, perched, ready to fall, stopping when he knew she had nothing left. The room dimmed, her hands and feet went numb. Something like terror filled her heart. She couldn't breathe.

"Sara," he whispered. He moved up her body at some point and hovered over her. She nodded, tears rolling down her cheeks. "Look at me." She shook her head.

"I can't." Her whisper filled the room. "I'm scared."

"Of what?" He kept working her flesh, nibbling, sucking, teasing, patting her clit, penetrating her with a finger, then pulling out. Her body hummed with erotic energy. She squirmed, tried to reach out for him. "I'm not going to hurt you. I've told you that before, lots of times. Why won't you just believe me?"

"I'm afraid to love you. I can't love anybody. And neither can you."

He covered her mouth, probed with his tongue, ran his hands up and down her naked body. When he broke their kiss, whispered in her ear before pulling her over on top of him. "Don't be afraid. Fall. I'll catch you. Let me catch you, please, baby. I need this."

With a tilt of his hips, he was inside her, making her gasp. "Sit up and ride me, baby. Like you want." He pushed her up so she sat, braced against his hard chest with one hand, gripping his thigh with the other.

"Oh dear God," she thought she yelled, but it came out a throaty whisper. Rocking her hips, she matched his rhythm as their bodies met, released, and met again. He cupped her breasts, pinched her nipples, making her move faster toward release. It roared up from the soles of her feet, bringing dark to the edge of her vision. "Jack!"

He groaned and gripped her thighs. "Yes. You can."

The room darkened as the exquisite beauty of a Jack induced orgasm rolled through her, making her forget everything but how much she loved him. He flipped them over, pinning her beneath him, pounding into her with a fierce purpose she loved.

She grabbed the headboard, using it to brace herself so she could lift her hips. "Fuck me hard Jack. I want it." He groaned, pounding into her until she sensed his release inside her. She wrapped her legs around him, never wanting it to end. But it did, as most perfect moments did. He took a shuddering breath and pulled out, flopping down beside her.

"Sleep," he muttered, pulling her close. "Let me hold you. No more fighting."

Sara grinned and tugged the duvet over them both. "I love you," she whispered. But he was already asleep.

Jack rolled over, smacking at the annoying animal that kept chirping near his head. "What the fuck?" He threw the clock across the room, which took care of the noise. But his head took up the reins and started clanging, his heart beating in time with the pain the way only a true bourbon hangover can do.

Groaning, he sat, noting the time. "Hey." He poked Sara's hip. She shifted and rolled onto her stomach. "What time is the first game?" She sat up, hair tumbled around her face.

"Oh, um, not until eleven. What time is it?"

"It's almost eight."

She turned over, tugged the sheet up to her chest.

"Oh shit, I gotta go. I have to get the girls to breakfast. Blake had them all night."

Jack groaned again when the sunlight streaming into the window hit his aching eyeballs. He watched her scrambling around for her clothes and recounted how badly he'd acted the night before. He'd been a full on idiot, made assumptions about what she'd done and with whom. Then solidified the idiocy by fucking her like an animal. He flopped back on the bed, pulled a pillow over his aching head.

"I'm sorry. I shouldn't have done that."

She sat next to him, but he moved away, embarrassed by his behavior. It was all too much. She was too much. He couldn't do this anymore.

"But, Jack, I thought..."

"It was a weak moment on my part. Won't happen again. I assure you."

She pulled away, anger flashing in her eyes.

Good. Anger, I can take.

After throwing the pillow across the room, he stumbled into the small kitchen, drank what felt like a gallon of life-giving water, then let his head droop between his shoulders.

This ends now, before we both end up lacerated one time too many.

He looked up to find her standing in the doorway, her jeans back on and wearing one of his shirts.

"You ripped mine, remember?" Her voice didn't bode well for reconciliation, but that worked for him.

"Sorry. Listen, Sara, I'm gonna end this now, okay? I'm sorry I brought the full-court pressure these last weeks. I thought we could make it work. I don't think we can."

She bit her lip, and he swallowed hard against the urge to pick her up again and take her to bed.

"Why though? You thought you caught me hitting on the soccer coach? So you go all Tarzan and fuck me 'til I scream then it's all, 'thanks, see ya later Sara?' Really?"

Her voice rose. He gritted his teeth and stared her down.

"Yeah. Guess so. You obviously needed something this weekend that didn't involve me. I show and you give me a nice ride. Now you're free to go, find your coach. I'll be fine."

"You're an amazing asshole, you know that? No, seriously, you turn the emotional valve off and one like it didn't matter one bit who's affected. You're done, because you misunderstand one scene and to hell with me. To hell with trying to explain anything. Not worth it—why bother? Fuck all of it." She threw up her hands.

He closed the gap between them, pressing her against the wall. She turned her face away, but he hissed into her neck.

"Sounds like a girl I used to know, back on the porch at her brother's lake house. She wouldn't let me explain anything that time, either." He shook with the effort not to kiss her. He wanted to so goddamn bad. But he released her, and she flounced out, unwilling or unable to respond. The door made a satisfying slam on her way out.

He dropped into a chair and stared at the door. What in the name of all he held dear had he done? Pushed her away with a load of crap about "finding the coach?"

Oh, right. That's good old Jack, ever suspicious, ever cynical, ever alone.

The trip home was hellish. Katie had popped a fever Sunday morning, and was crying, sniveling, asking for Uncle Jack, refusing Sara's help. Blake hovered, worried, but that pissed her off even more.

She and Jack hadn't exchanged two civil words the rest of the weekend, keeping it short and as hurtful as possible. By the time she climbed into her SUV Sunday, after letting Katie ride home with Jack, she was quivering with stress. She pulled into Ann Arbor around seven p.m. after getting a speeding ticket on top of everything else.

She took the longest shower on the planet, wrapped up in a robe, poured some wine, and flopped onto her couch. Refusing to spare another tear on Jack and all their missed opportunities, she shoved all thoughts of him out of her mind.

Determined to find that place in her head and her life where she could exist without Jack, or thoughts of Jack, or memories of Jack, she opened her laptop to peruse what crises had arisen in her absence. She tapped out a few replies, and after a couple of hours, refilled her wine glass and looked at her non-work emails. One of them was an invitation from one of the moms for a Memorial Day cookout for the team.

She answered that she and Katie would be there and got a near simultaneous reply. "What about Jack?"

Fingers curled over the keyboard, she squeezed her eyes shut, willing herself to be calm. Without answering, she picked up her phone and made herself insane by scrolling through her last exchange with the man in question. The one where she'd invited him over for a nice quiet dinner, and her proposal.

The rings were still in the box, sitting on the side table where she'd left them Friday. They shone in the next of black velvet, mocking her when she opened the box with a shaking hand.

Well, one thing's for sure. I know how he feels all those times I rejected his offer of marital jewelry.

With a loud curse, she threw the ring box and her damn phone across the room, watching in satisfaction as it shattered against the wall. The box bounced and landed on the dark hardwood floor, unscathed.

Making a mental note to get to the phone store in the morning for a replacement, she turned back to her laptop. "You'll have to ask Jack yourself, sorry," she said in reply before hitting send.

Blake pinged her on Google chat. "Hey your phone's dead."

"Yeah. I killed it."

"You okay?"

"I'm the opposite of okay. That man is going to be the death of me. You and Dad were right. I should have listened."

"No, we weren't. You're being obtuse. But I get it. I understand the need to guard yourself against being hurt. I think it's time you and he got past that. But you have to decide what's best, not me or Dad. I'm here for you, you know that."

"I do. Thanks."

She saw Jack sign in on Google, and then ignore her even though he could see she was on there too. Her fingers hovered, itching, needing to reach out, but she wouldn't give him the satisfaction. Never again. Of course, her phone was dead and if there was an issue with Katie, he couldn't reach her. She typed quickly.

"Katie okay?"

"Yes. Fever's gone. She's in bed. I'll take her to school tomorrow."

"Okay."

His next words surprised her.

"I'm sorry."

"So am I."

She turned the damn thing off and went to bed. When she woke, her pillow clung to her face, wet from tears.

Chapter Twenty-Five

Sara sipped her beer and watched the pack of kids run through the picnic area, across the open field, and into the woods. Katie led the pack, the usual set of bruises on her arms and legs prominent in her shorts and swimsuit top. The girl had stayed just under the weather all week, but was never sick enough to warrant another doctor visit.

Sara leaned back in her camp chair, unable to engage in much conversation with the surrounding parents. She wished she hadn't agreed to come. Jack wasn't here, which both disappointed and aggravated her. Katie's words about the matter hadn't helped.

"He has a fancy date tonight, Mama. He showed me his monkey suit. But I told him it wasn't a real monkey suit 'cause it didn't have a tail or ears."

"A fancy date, huh? With who?" she'd asked, although she'd known.

"Shannon," the girl had said. "But he says it's something he has to do, that he'd promised her he'd do and he always keeps his promises, right Mama?"

"Yes. Right." She'd kissed the girl's forehead, frowning when her mom-radar-lips sensed heat. "You're hot again, baby. Let me take your temperature." But the girl had run to her room, unwilling to miss the picnic. Sara had dosed her with some ibuprofen and chalked it up to her ongoing cold. The girl was the biggest social butterfly and would have to be peeled away from attending a team picnic, especially since they were going to play more soccer.

At one point during the long afternoon, she spotted Katie at the edge of the crowd, bent at the waist. She stood and made her way through parents—all staring at her. Thanks to her embarrassing screw up that had involved getting "caught" with the coach at the tournament. Fucking gossips.

"Honey? What's wrong?"

"Don't know Mommy. My tummy hurts really bad all of a sudden." But she straightened, her eyes bright. Sara took in her filthy face, covered with mustard, chocolate, and God only knew what else.

"You want to go home?" Her mom radar pinged, making her wince. "Let's go, okay?"

"No, I'm fine. Mateo's gonna take us over to the field to play a game. I gotta play mom! I'm fine." Sara stepped away, reluctant and now on alert.

"Well, if it happens again..." But the girl was gone in a whirl of denim and pink—her second favorite color after purple.

Sara sat in the crowd, feeling utterly alone. The kids played, lead by Matteo, who had, with reason, avoided her like the plague. They distracted her as she sipped her second beer. Lila sat and tried to chat with her, but gave up after Sara apologized and said she wasn't in a mood to talk.

After a few more minutes, a shout made her glance up. The shout was no different from any other, but it set her teeth on edge in a way that demanded her attention. She stood and watched Mateo running towards her, Katie clutched in his arms.

Great, another busted ankle or hurt wrist or...

"Sara! Get the car. We have to take her to the hospital."

"What?"

"Just get the damn car!"

On autopilot, she brought the car to a screeching halt in front of him. He piled the girl's unconscious body into the back, cradling her in his arms. The family stood, silent. "Go! Go! Hurry!" She did, teeth clenched as Mateo soothed and tried to cajole the girl out of her faint. "Dear God, she's burning up with fever, Sara! Go faster."

By the time she pulled into the University emergency department, her teeth were chattering with fear, and she could barely get out of the car. A team of doctors and nurses hustled out and piled Katie's tiny body onto a huge stretcher.

Jack. She needed Jack.

She lost sight of Katie at one point, and stood in the middle of the busy emergency room chaos, tears streaming down her face. When she heard a familiar voice, she had to grab the wall to keep from collapsing.

"Craig," she whispered, and ran around the corner. His eyes widened, and he handed a computer tablet to a nurse, catching her before she fell. "Katie..." She didn't get another word in. He handed her off to the same nurse, and dashed away, bursting into the triage area with a quiet calm that made everyone take a step back.

Craig gave orders and worked around her daughter's lifeless looking body. The sight of so many people hovering, then the sound of a loud alarm which brought even more doctors to the room, made her want to throw up, or die. She sank to the floor, against the wall, as the staff swirled around her, as if she weren't even there.

When they got her stabilized, Craig came out and pulled her to her feet.

"Sara, listen. Katie's appendix has burst. I have about three minutes to get her into surgery to keep her from drowning in her body's own poison. Here, sign this." Sara's hand shook so badly she couldn't hold the pen.

She heard him before she saw him. Jack barreled around the corner, in full black tie, the lovely Shannon trailing behind. He gripped Sara's arm.

"Where is she?"

Craig gave him the same story.

Minutes. Drowning. Poison.

He signed the paper. A nurse started to protest, to say only Sara had the authority, but the room's buzz had reached a fever pitch. Arms reached out to ease her into a seat.

"He can sign." Craig's voice pierced her fog as she stumbled over to the bed, needing to touch her. But her hands hovered. Her daughter looked so small in the giant bed, hooked up to machines that kept her alive.

Then Jack was at her side. "What has she been doing? She's covered in dirt and bruises." The girl flinched. A nurse spoke to Jack.

"She hears you, Dad. Keep talking to her."

Jack's wild stare caught hers. Anger and helplessness oozed from his every pore. He glared over her shoulder. "Him?" She turned and saw Matteo standing in the hallway, in his soccer gear, head down.

"Yeah, Jack, he saved her. Got her here on time. Fuck you and your monkey suit and over-dressed date."

"Mom, Dad, can we focus on the little girl for a minute?"

"I'm not her..." Jack started, then stopped. Tears dripped down Sara's face onto the bed.

"Jack, I need you to donate blood." Craig had another paper in hand. "Katie needs a transfusion and you're the only one... with her blood type." Jack stared at him.

"Uh, okay, how do you know that... I mean... where? When?"

"Here, now." Craig pointed him towards a nurse. He turned and caught Sara's gaze again. The expression on face—a mix of terror and something like understanding—made her suck in a breath. "We've got to move her to surgery. The staff will bring you up." Craig kissed her cheek, then disappeared down the hall and into a giant elevator with her baby, her heart, her only reason for living.

Jack's daughter.

She squeezed her eyes shut, relieved that the fact of Katie's parentage was no longer anyone's secret.

She flopped into a chair and sent texts to Blake, Julie, and her parents, who were down in Florida, before sinking into a chair. A nurse brought her water. After about thirty minutes or maybe an hour, she had no real sense of time anymore, she spotted Jack at the far end of the hall, rolling his shirt sleeve down. Shannon spoke to him. He shook his head. The woman seemed agitated, but he put an arm around her and guided her to the door.

A few minutes later, he reappeared alone and stood, leaning against the wall opposite the bank of chairs where she sat.

"Appendicitis has pretty distinct symptoms." His voice curled inside her head like smoke. "You didn't notice? Too busy with the new boy toy?" She rose, and without a word, followed the nurse upstairs to the surgical waiting room.

They sat at opposite ends of the waiting room, alternatively glaring at or ignoring each for the next hour and a half. At one point, she shivered so violently she thought her teeth would rattle out of her head. She looked up at a tap on her shoulder. Jack was holding out his tuxedo coat. When she looked away, he dropped it in her lap muttering words that sounded like "stubborn" and "impossible" as she slipped her arms into it, sucking in breaths of him, soothed in spite of herself.

Craig reappeared, his face grim. She stayed seated and let him come to her. Jack moved to sit beside her.

"It must have been a slow rupture. It happens. You said she'd had off and on fevers, flu-like symptoms, for a couple of weeks, right?" Sara nodded. Jack grabbed her hand, but she hardly felt his touch. "She has peritonitis, inflammation of the stomach lining, because of the rupture that none of us caught. I saw her myself." He looked at Jack. "So don't blame yourselves—or each other. Appendicitis is one of the hardest things to diagnose."

He ran a hand over his face.

"She's stable, on tons of strong antibiotics, but the next twenty-four hours." Sara let out a sob. Jack's hand tightened on hers.

"She lost blood inside her abdomen, which is why I wanted the transfusion." He looked at Jack. "You saved her life with that donation."

Air. Sara needed air.

No. She needed to see Katie. To hold her.

She stared at Craig, panic rising in every pore of her body. "Why did they have to, um, revive her?"

"She was in septic shock by the time you got here. Her blood pressure was practically zero."

Jack put his head in his hands. She stared at him a second before acknowledging that his shoulders were shaking.

"Sara!" The sound of Blake's voice made her jump up and run to him.

Jack stood slowly.

"Where is she? I want to be with her." His deep voice rumbled in her ears.

"She's being moved to recovery. You and Sara are the only ones allowed in there, but not for about fifteen minutes. She'll stay there for us to monitor her blood pressure for a while."

Without a word to anyone, Jack stalked out of the room with its soothing blue décor, soft chairs, and subtle music. Maureen joined Blake, Rob and Julie in the hall, but he walked past them. The flow of tears blurring her vision of Jack's retreating back. She stepped out of Blake's embrace and started for him, but the room dimmed, then blurred. Rob grabbed her before she hit the floor, then everything went as dark as the jacket Jack had given her to wear.

Walk. Forward motion. Positive action. Get out. Somewhere out of here.

The mantra played in Jack's head, propelling him down the hallway. He saw nothing but the set of doors in the distance. On his best day, hospitals made him nervous. But today, with the multiple stunning news flashes he'd been offered, had no equal.

He spotted a men's room once he'd made it through the swinging double doors, shouldered his way in, and sat in a stall, fully dressed, pressing his pounding head against the metal stall door.

For all his blustering proclamations a few years ago, he'd not been convinced the girl was his, other than the fact that he helped raise her.

Which should be enough. Her green eyes and darkening hair didn't help her look more like anything, except more like her mother. He sucked in a deep breath.

"Jack?" Mo's voice came from outside the main door.

"Go away," he shouted, but his raw throat only managed a whisper.

She walked in anyway, and knocked on the stall door. When he continued to ignore her, she climbed up on the toilet in the next stall and peered down at him.

"How do you know I'm not in here needing privacy?"

"I'll take my chances. You can see her now. Sara passed out. She's lying on the couch in the waiting room. Katie's awake, though, and asking for you."

He launched himself out the door and down the hall in seconds, not even aware of his feet touching the floor. She needed him.

His daughter.

Craig held open a door and guided him in.

"She's weak and her throat probably hurts from the tube, but she stabilized quickly, so I took it out to eliminate the possibility of any more infection. Once she went septic, it opened up her immune system to all sorts of..."

Jack glared at him.

"Already too much information, Doctor Craig, but thank you. Thank you for saving her." He hesitated, then gave the other man a tight hug.

"Oh, okay then." Craig patted his back, then nodded into the room. Jack took a deep breath. His baby girl half sat, propped up, tubes, lines hanging off her arms. His ears buzzed so loudly he had a brief moment to be thankful that he was in a hospital where they could deal when he had a heart attack.

A hand on his arm steadied him. His sister's deep blue gaze connected with his. "Go. She needs you."

He nodded and pushed the door open. Beeps and other strange sounds, plus the plastic, antiseptic odor of hospital assaulted his senses. He stayed frozen in place. Her eyes moved under lids that seemed thin and fragile. Her face was gaunt, bruised-looking.

"She's so... small." His Kate was tough, with a smart mouth to match her mother's, a pink and purple-wearing tomboy of the nth degree. "Dear God, please..." He croaked out before sitting in the chair near her head. His entire body shook.

Be strong. She needs you.

He clenched his fists, then released them and put a hand over hers. The chill emanating from her skin frightened him. He glanced at the many monitors bleeping and ringing.

"Mommy?" Her voice sounded papery thin as her eyes fluttered open.

Jack took a breath and touched her cheek. "No honey. It's me."

"My throat hurts. My head hurts. Can you turn the light down?" A nurse obliged, making the already dim room more so.

A tear slipped down her cheek. Jack stood, then sat again, antsy, more stressed than he'd ever been. Maureen slipped in and whispered in his ear. "Craig told me to tell you to calm down. Her heartbeat's getting too fast. You need to talk to her, get her to relax."

He gulped, swallowing the huge lump that had taken up residence in this throat.

"Get Sara," he whispered to his sister. "Throw water on her to wake her up if you have to. I don't care, just get her in here."

She gave him a squeeze and left. Katie had started crying in earnest, her ravaged throat unable to make the sobbing noises any louder than a squeak. He looked up at Craig, who was standing on the other side of the glass wall. The man's almost imperceptible nod gave him strength. Wiping his eyes to clear them, he reached deep, found a firm tone, free of the wobbly emotion coursing through him.

"Scooch over. I'm gonna stretch out here with you. That okay?"

She nodded, reduced to sniffles as the nurse helped him adjust all her wires and tubes. Parking himself with one foot still on the floor, he gathered his daughter in his arms and held her close, rocking and her, kissing her hair. The action soothed them both.

By the time she'd fallen into a fitful sleep, Jack's eyes burned with unshed tears. He settled her back on the pillows and took a seat, laid his aching head on the side of her bed and kept stroking her arm until he was startled awake by a hand on his hair.

"Daddy?" she whispered, making the tears he'd held back for the last hours release and roll down his face as he nodded, speechless at her existence, much less that she'd figured it out. "I knew it." She smiled and grabbed his hand, threading her fingers through his, her flushed face wet with more tears. Craig gave him a thumbs-up through the glass.

Sara followed Mo across the hall. Everything in her screamed for escape, to run away, start this fucking day all over again—hell, start her entire year over. Maybe the last decade—starting when she met Jack Gordon the first time.

Blake and Rob touched her arm. Mo gave her a quick squeeze, but she didn't feel any of it.

Craig stood at the window of a recovery room before he turned and nearly ran into her. There was no mistaking the tears standing in his eyes. She clutched his arm.

"She's still okay?"

"Yeah, she's good. Go on, be with him." The long look he gave her sent a deeper message. One she caught but couldn't credit. She pushed the door open. Watched as her daughter put her hand on Jack's head—Jack Gordon, the man she'd loved since the moment she laid eyes on him. Katie said, "Daddy" and "I knew it."

The tears rolling down Jack's face, the way he held her—their—daughter's hand, hardened her resolve. She shook all over, but made a decision at that moment. One she'd never regret.

She walked over and put a hand on Jack's shoulder. He glanced up at her, worry mixed with relief in his deep blue eyes. She pulled him to his feet, wrapped herself around him, and held him tight.

"Don't let go," he whispered into her hair. "Don't ever let me go. Please. Sara, I can't lose you both."

"I won't." She lifted her face to his. "Ever."

Epilogue

••••

SARA SHIFTED ON THE couch, let the blanket slide to the floor, and studied the dancing flames in the fireplace. From somewhere in the still not-quite renovated house, Katie shrieked with delight and pounded down the hall with the scrabble of dog toenails right behind her. The two collided in a happy heap in the living room, the slobbering puppy climbing all over his beloved mistress.

"Take him outside before he pees again," Jack's voice floated out from the kitchen. "Sara, do you need more water?" She shook her head, suddenly overcome with a bout of extreme happiness. She wiped at her eyes. All seemed as though all she did anymore was cry at the oddest moments.

He stuck his head around the doorway. They'd moved into the new house, on an acre and a half of prime real estate in the Ann Arbor Hills neighborhood a week ago. A retro-sixties raised ranch, with tons of exposed wood and an old kitchen to match, it suited them all perfectly. Mostly because it was exactly the opposite of where they came from. Jack already had the plans drawn up for the kitchen and bath remodel, plus a huge basement upgrade.

The whole thing made her tired, but then again, so did breathing these days.

"I'm sick of sitting here, Jack."

"Don't you dare get up. I mean it." He wandered in, clad in flannel pants and a t-shirt.

"Sit with me, distract me or something. I'm going nuts." He plopped down beside her, handing her a glass of lemon-infused water, and put a hand on her belly. "I hate being pregnant. I blame you for all of this misery, John Patrick, up to and including my extreme bitchiness."

"Yeah? What's your excuse when you aren't knocked up?" He smiled and kissed her, then flipped on the television. She sighed and rubbed her aching back before picking up the framed photo next to the couch.

There was a montage of images from the July wedding on the Lake Michigan beach she'd chosen from the thousands of shots the photographer provided. She, Blake, Rob and Lila with the little girls in their sundresses. Jack and Maureen. Katie and her cousins all laughing at something off camera. Jack and her with her parents, who seemed relaxed and happy for a change.

A small shot of Craig sitting with Katie in his lap, Suzanne in the chair next to him, all three of them wearing Ray-Bans and cool expressions. The middle photo, though, was her favorite. The one that got her every time. She and Jack caught in an unscripted moment, arms around each other's waists, staring into each other's eyes.

She grabbed his hand and threaded her fingers through his. The heavy but simple matching platinum bands they wore made her smile. She'd surprised him with them a week after Katie came home from the hospital. The moment she knew she was pregnant again, thanks to that night in Traverse City. A fact she'd kept from him long enough for her to wrap her mind around it.

She'd kept the news for the right moment, and the look in his eyes, captured forever in that one photo with the west Michigan sun setting behind them, was one she'd carry with her forever.

"Shove over, you're like an oven," He moved his legs away, grinning at her. Katie came back in and ran down the hall to her new room with the dog.

"I heard this thing about orgasm," she whispered in her husband's ear. He raised an eyebrow and tugged her close again, running a hand up the swell of her belly to cup a breast.

"What's that? That I am the king giver of same?"

"Well, besides that. I also heard that it can bring on labor. And I'm sick of being pregnant, so what do you say we try the theory?" She nibbled his ear.

"I'm never one to turn down a challenge." He stood, and in one motion, picked her up.

"Jesus Christ, Jack, put me down. You'll break your back."

He pretended to stumble, groaned, then stood straight, his smile sending a bolt of happiness straight to her soul. "I'm good. And so will you be, in a few short minutes."

She wrapped her arms around his and kissed him, ignoring Katie's protests of "Ew, gross."

"Mom and Dad need a nap," Jack called over his shoulder. "Pretend there is a Do Not Disturb sign on the door." He grinned at the girl as she made her way out to the television. "Now, about that theory..." He nuzzled her neck after laying her carefully on the bed.

"Tell me first," she insisted.

"No, you first," he said as he unbuttoned her shirt, kissing every inch of skin he exposed.

"Fine. I love you Jack."

He grinned before lowering his lips to her flesh. "I know, baby. I know."

"Your turn," she said with a loud sigh of satisfaction.

He leaned on his elbow beside her, his fingers trailing across her belly before joining hers and twining them together. She grinned when the baby chose that moment to give a healthy kick to their joined hands.

"I will never get used to that," Jack said, rubbing the tiny heel or fist or whatever it was gently until it settled back into place. When he reached up to stroke her flushed face, his eyes were dark as midnight, and shining with something she damn knew were tears. She smiled and touched his face. They'd done this, and while it was far from perfect, she was so happy even the struggles, arguments and frustrations were manageable. All part and parcel of a real, modern marriage.

"I love you, Sara. With everything I have."

"I know, baby. I know," she said. "But um... have you forgotten why we're in here?" She pointed downward, over the giant swell of her stomach.

He grinned, the sight of which always made her breath catch in her throat, and got back to work.

The End

• • • •

WOO HOO! JACK AND SARA together! I know I put you through a lot but that was definitely worth it, don't you think? Ok, now...it's time to tell Blake's story. Be sure to download DUAL AGENCY next and dive into a sexy, poignant novel about love unexpected, love requited, and love that endures.

• • • •

HERE'S A QUICK PEEK to tempt you....it's from the middle of the book, when Blake meets Rob.

• • • •

THIS BOOK STARTS WITH Rob's backstory, how he met Jack, then reveals Blake and Suzanne's relationship before these two finally meet each other. It was one of my favorite books to write in the series. I hope you enjoy it too.

• • • •

ROB WAS SCHEDULED TO work the Taste of the Midwest beer fest, doing pairings with some of the bigger breweries featuring a few of their dishes, both at the restaurant after the festival hours and at the event itself. His aggravation after a recent brief and unsatisfactory conversation with Jack about Suzanne was making him antsy. He'd tried to call her, see how she was, but kept getting voicemail. The texts he sent went unanswered.

Just as well, he supposed. He'd cut them off for the last two years. Why would they think he wanted back in now? But the twitchy, quick-tempered sensation remained, and had resulted in an epic argument with the hostess he'd been fucking, ending with her telling him he could take his bullshit attitude and shove it up his ass.

He hadn't missed her, which told him a lot about himself and his deep capacity for shallowness. After glaring into the rearview mirror before climbing out of his jeep and entering the crowd of beer drinkers, he had to acknowledge that he didn't like himself much lately. While he looked great on the outside, never healthier or more fit, he felt like shit on the inside, and didn't know what he could do to fix it.

He ran the midday gig in the food tent, then wandered around, tasting and greeting some friends in the brewery business. It was always a fun group. He missed it. Letting a pleasant buzz settle in his head, and rebuffing a couple of hot but drunk girls, he took a seat at one of the round tables to the side of the Michigan beer tent.

He didn't notice the someone slumped in a chair opposite him at first. When the guy looked up, Rob determined that he was eye-rolling shit-faced drunk. Not to mention incredibly attractive. His body shifted into high alert for the first time in ages as he observed the young man's lean, fit torso, highlighted by the soft looking plain black t-shirt.

The guy looked at him, attempting to focus his eyes—which were the most amazing shade of green Rob had ever seen. The extreme unhappiness in them hit him in the guts. He moved to the chair closer, putting a hand on the stranger's arm. "Hey, you okay?" The guy flinched and glared up at Rob through a flop of dark blond hair. The man blew at it, but it settled back where it was partially obscuring one of those deep green eyes. "No. Thanks. I'm not." He sat back and stared up at the darkening sky. "Go 'way." He turned, showing Rob his profile.

The line of his jaw, covered with dark stubble, begged for Rob's touch. That shaggy, messy hair screamed for fingers through it. He clenched his fists, cleared his throat, and willed his body down from the lusty ledge. The kid was drunk, needed help and to sober up, not to be hit on by a horny older man.

"Listen." Rob put a hand on his shoulder. The man's skin was hot under the thin t-shirt. He looked at Rob's hand, then back into his eyes, making Rob's breath catch in his throat. "I'm Rob. Why don't you let me..."

The man leaned into him, giving Rob a whiff of beer, light cologne, and sunscreen. He put a hand on Rob's thigh, making him almost jump out of his skin. He'd never in his life picked up a man, drunk or otherwise, in a public place, much less a beer festival.

This young man, so near him right now, exuded the sort of needy vibe that struck him hard between the eyes. Rob was no caretaker, never had been. He was too much of a loner to be in tune with what others required from him. But an odd, almost woozy sensation of pure desire to help washed over Rob. He needed to get him somewhere safe to sleep off the drunk and get past whatever hurt had gotten him to this point. It almost suffocated Rob with its urgency.

The guy squinted up at him. "I'm Blake. And you..." He squeezed Rob's leg, his face too close to Rob's own for comfort. "You are... really tall." He squinted a moment, as if focusing on Rob for the first time.

Then he let go and lurched to his feet, stumbling and tripping past folding chairs in his haste to get out of the tent. Rob followed him, helped him up after he'd dropped to his hand and knees and puked on the grass and guided him into a waiting taxi.

"Okay Blake. I'm Rob." He crouched down on the sidewalk to be eye-to-eye, marveling again at the deep green that met his gaze. "Where should I send you?"

Blake gripped his arm, sending a shock wave through Rob's entire body. Blake must have sensed it, too. He let go fast, staring at his own hand, then up at Rob with a childlike, innocent puzzlement that made Rob gulp. "Uh, dunno. Someone else did hotel stuff. I'm... too..."

The decision Rob made at that moment was one he'd look back on and thank god for, but which made him doubt his sanity at the moment. He shoved Blake's floppy form across the back seat and climbed in, giving the taxi driver his home address. Blake slumped against the far door, already snoring.

What in the name of all that is potential jailbait are you doing, Freitag? Picking up boys at the beer fest? Nice.

He shook his head, lifted his arm and tugged the young man off the window, loving the perfect way he fit into his side. "Sorry," Blake mumbled.

When they arrived at his building, he jostled Blake out and into the elevator, hating himself for how much he loved touching him. He stared at the two of them in the elevator door's reflection.

"Thanks," Blake slurred, sounding more like "shlanks" before Rob lowered him to the large leather couch. Rob put a hand on Blake's hair, touched his rough jaw and acknowledged the slow loosening of the vise he'd had around his chest for the past year or two. Blake mumbled some more, rolled onto his side, and commenced snoring again. Rob pulled off his shoes and tried not to stare at the obvious physical perfection that hid under Blake's faded jeans before covering him with a blanket.

Cut the shit, you dirty old man. Let the kid sleep it off, then point him wherever he needs to go. The end.

But Rob sat longer than he realized, watching Blake sleep.

And I know that you're going to want the rest of this series! Read in this order:
Floor Time
Sweat Equity
Closing Costs
Dual Agency
Conditional Offer
Escalation Clause
Mutual Release
Backup Offer
PLUS the Jack Gordon Prequel: HOUSE RULES!

And don't miss GOOD FAITH—a Stewart Realty series affiliated novel that is an epic leap into the second generation. It is not a romance but it contains several romantic storylines.

• • • •

IF YOU SUBSCRIBE TO my newsletter, you'll get all the awesome updates that I have planned for the coming year, including multiple novellas from this series, some of which you can ONLY get if you are a Liz Newz Subscriber!

Go to lizcrowe.com to subscribe.

And be sure to snag your free Stewart Realty Prequel: HOUSE RULES when you subscribe! This is EXCLUSIVE to Liz newsletter subscribers only!

Milton Keynes UK
Ingram Content Group UK Ltd.
UKHW020914140524
442690UK00015B/627